~~Jenny Q,~~ Stitched Up!

Pauline McLynn lives in Dublin with her husband, Richard, and two cats named Brenda and Alice. She used to have other cats too – Mutt, Geoff, Noel, Brendan, Snubby and Geezee. When she was growing up in Galway, in the west of Ireland, her family had dogs – Roberta, Lady Pink Weasel, Dennis and TD. Her brothers used to call her 'verucca head' and 'hook nose' (serio) but they don't do that any more, at least not to her face, which is good. She has a wonky, crackly right knee from doing Irish dancing (probably the wrong way!) when she was younger. Pauline still loves performing and is now an award-winning actor, perhaps best known for playing the role of Mrs Doyle in *Father Ted* and Libby Croker in *Shameless*. She is also very good at knitting and has written eight other novels, but *Jenny Q, Stitched Up!* is her first book for teenagers.

spinebreakers.co.uk

Jenny Q, Stitched Up!

PAULINE McLYNN

PUFFIN BOOKS

Published by the Penguin Group
Penguin Books Ltd, 80 Strand, London WC2R 0RL, England
Penguin Group (USA) Inc., 375 Hudson Street, New York, New York 10014, USA
Penguin Group (Canada), 90 Eglinton Avenue East, Suite 700, Toronto, Ontario, Canada M4P 2Y3
(a division of Pearson Penguin Canada Inc.)
Penguin Ireland, 25 St Stephen's Green, Dublin 2, Ireland
(a division of Penguin Books Ltd)
Penguin Group (Australia), 250 Camberwell Road, Camberwell, Victoria 3124, Australia
(a division of Pearson Australia Group Pty Ltd)
Penguin Books India Pvt Ltd, 11 Community Centre, Panchsheel Park, New Delhi – 110 017, India
Penguin Group (NZ), 67 Apollo Drive, Rosedale, Auckland 0632, New Zealand
(a division of Pearson New Zealand Ltd)
Penguin Books (South Africa) (Pty) Ltd, Block D, Rosebank Office Park, 181 Jan Smuts Avenue,
Parktown North, Gauteng 2193, South Africa

Penguin Books Ltd, Registered Offices: 80 Strand, London WC2R 0RL, England

puffinbooks.com

First published 2012
001 – 10 9 8 7 6 5 4 3 2 1

Text copyright © Pauline McLynn, 2012
Illustrations copyright © Kate Jenkins and Puffin Books, 2012
All rights reserved

The moral right of the author has been asserted

Set in 12/18pt Gill Sans
Typeset by Palimpsest Book Production Ltd, Falkirk, Stirlingshire
Printed in Great Britain by Clays Ltd, St Ives plc

British Library Cataloguing in Publication Data
A CIP catalogue record for this book is available from the British Library

ISBN: 978-0-141-34103-3

www.greenpenguin.co.uk

MIX
Paper from
responsible sources
FSC® C018179

Penguin Books is committed to a sustainable
future for our business, our readers and our planet.
This book is made from Forest Stewardship
Council™ certified paper.

ALWAYS LEARNING   **PEARSON**

For Sarah Webb, who told me I could do this,
so then I had to,
and Paddy O'Doherty, who helped me
along the writing road

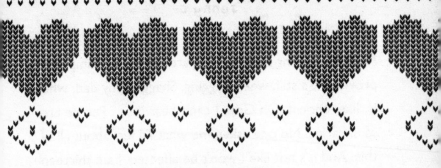

DIZASSO

Right, here's how things are, and I warn you from the outset that this is ugly. Here goes – my parents have done the icky thing (the Big Icky) and I am going to have a new brother or sister. I am in a sweat even saying it, feeling faint. My mother is pregnant.

I can tell you for nothing that this is most unexpected for all concerned, and very most certainly totally out of the blue for me (= understatement of the year). URG. And pregnant is not a *lovely* word, either, is it? It's not pretty, like flowery aprons and baking. PREG–NANT. I am *so* not loving the sound of that, at ALL. It's not something I want to even think about. It makes me, I dunno, *queasy*. I mean, really, at their age you'd think they'd have calmed down. It's just so, well, SHAMEFUL. And now it's going to be plain for all the world to see.

My mum is going to be walking around with a bump that proves she's still, well, shagging. Shagging my dad, who is, like, *ancient*. Oh God, I can't bear it . . . People are so uncaring. No one asked me what I'd feel about all of this. And it's not like I won't be affected. I am thirteen and about to become the butt of all Oakdale jokes . . .*

HOW COULD THEY?

I'd call Dixie for a meeting to discuss this but I cannot face her crowing and picking over the situation. She may be my Bestest but she is also a mere human and there are some things that are just too delicious for any friend not to enjoy and I reckon this is one of them. I will have to plan how to tell her with extreme care if I am to avoid further dizassos.

As far as family goes (and I wish they would!), I already have a brother, Dermot, and he's plenty to be going on with. He's sixteen now and thinks he's God's gift to the world. He plays a lot of rugby so his name has morphed into 'Dermo' because all rugby-heads are Beno or Domo or Thicko or whatever(o) – it's like some weird(o) rule they have with names. He's started wearing shred-

---

* That or his latest antiperspirant isn't working or has a totally tragic smell.

ded clothes and I think he's stopped washing,[†] so he's very noticeable. Moody too. I don't need extra attention being brought on us Quinns as a family. We're freakish enough as it is.

Now, I've been well aware of how all the ickiness happens since I was a tiny kid. Our house always had those pop-up books with men's and women's bits in 3D so I was under no illusion as to what went where. And for what it's worth I didn't like those books half as much as the ones with fairy tales in – there's only so much anatomy any child should have to look at. Then Mum took it upon herself to clarify a few things when I was a bit older. It went along the lines of 'the man and woman needed to be deeply in love to make babies' and all that. You'd think the Seed passed from the man to the woman kind of invisibly and magically the way she described it – I SWEAR that's what she tried to fob off on me. After all the educational books I'd had to endure as a child, who did she think she was kidding?

So when we got our official Biology books at school from Miss Greene, and on page 121 there were (flat,

---

† That or his latest antiperspirant isn't working or has a totally tragic smell.

3

non pop-up) diagrams of men's bits and women's bits and a full explanation of all that was involved, I took the opportunity to storm home and ask: 'Are you honestly telling me that people do it like the dogs on the street?'

Mum almost smiled.‡ She read the piece and said, 'Yes, Jen, that looks like an accurate enough description of it all.'

'So much for love,' I announced, all indignant (though I am still secretly hoping that there is something in all that love stuff). I didn't get to say anything more because I heard a snuffling and realized there was someone else in the kitchen. It was my gran. She had stuffed part of a teacloth into her mouth to stifle the sound of her laughing and she nearly choked on it.

And to think that's how I got made too . . . I'm feeling faint again . . . Choccy bicky time for Jenny Q. Actually, it's Emergency Kit Kat⁶ time, which is major crisis diversion and not to be taken lightly. I am heading down to the kitchen to raid my stash of chocolate, the one truly reliable thing in the Quinn household.

‡ I shizz you not - she wasn't in the least bit embarrassed!
⁶ The Kit Kat is my snack of choice as it is the greatest ever invented - FACT.

4

Thank goodness it is still the school holidays and as such I do not have to confront the HORROR that is my class for another few weeks. They could surely not help but snigger at my obvious predicament now that I am the Ideal of Ickiness, thanks to my parents. Come to think of it, 'Ireland' is only two letters away from being 'Ickland', so we had a lucky escape. I have no doubt that I would be crowned the Rose of Ickland under current circumstances.

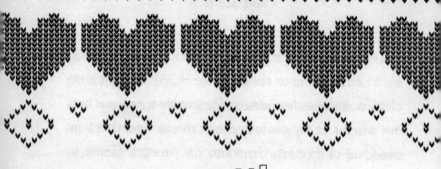

NIX!

To add to my annoyance (as if that's needed), Dixie (*supposed* Bestest) is in the kitchen with Mum when I get downstairs. They're both snaffling anything and everything covered in chocolate. I try a reverse move the minute I see them so that I can regroup my thoughts and get a plan of action together but they're on to me immediately and I am trapped in their gaze.

I think they've got through all of the Kit Kats, so I'm probably going to have to settle for a blinkin' Wagon Wheel or some such, and it may not be up to taking the edge off the awfulness of what's happening here. I'm getting a v v uncomfortable feeling about the way they're smiling at me.

'HULlo,' I say to Dix, all pointed as in 'What are

you doing here with my mum and not upstairs with me discussing major life developments?' kinda thing.

She's all innocent and beaming and then gets me with the word I just *know* is coming, the word that takes things up a notch in the Jen Quinn Cringestakes. 'Congratulations,' she says (or rather, 'Congratulations,' she *lies*!).

ARGH, Dixie *knows*, and I wasn't the one to tell her. This is *not* good. I *so* don't want to be here. Things cannot get any worse, surely.

They do.* That's the major lesson you learn in life as you get older: as bad as things are, they can certainly get worse, especially if your name is Jennifer Quinn.

Dermot and his friends pile in, including Stevie Lee Bolton, who is a god, end of. He's got these deep brown eyes that a girl could lose herself in. Today he's in a white T-shirt that shows off his tan and a pair of totally fabulous camouflage cargo shorts. He makes my knees want to stop doing their job and my breathing goes wonky when he's around.

I am feeling hotter and hotter now, close to boiling, and I'm hoping my face isn't all red and blotchy. Why

---

* Well, OF COURSE they do.

didn't I slick on some lip gloss before I came down the stairs? I have a rule never to leave or enter a room without doing that, and the latest one is strawberry flavoured and I'm hoping it'll make people think my breath is always fruity too. (In a good way, not fruity like Mr Fox, our Mathematics teacher, who has, well, fox breath and seems to be decomposing.) But I have not glossed. This is how scrambled my poor head is with this family and all that comes with it. Thankfully I am wearing a summery skirt instead of my usual jeans, which Dixie persuaded me to buy because she said it's 'on trend', so Stevie Lee Bolton will at least think I am at the cutting edge of fashion = brief PHEW for that.

Maybe I'm adopted, I suddenly think. Yes, that would offer a plausible[†] explanation as to why I am clearly so different from the rest of the mentalists[‡] in this house. I file this idea with all of the others like it in my brain, because it's not the first time I've had this notion.

[†] 'Plausible' is a good word and I'm going to write it into my Great Words That Should Be Used More Often notebook.

[‡] There are MANY mentalists involved.

Then my friend Uggs arrives, and it's all 'Eugene, my man' and high fives from the older boys, which makes him preen. Although he is my friend, Dermot will actually speak to him because he is also our neighbour. And a boy. But all I can think is that Uggs being here means Gyp cannot be far behind.

She's not.

She races in, barking, and attaches her sticky-outy teeth to my ankle and starts to chew. I shake my leg a bit to get her off but she's tenacious today and all that happens is I teeter, *alarmingly*. I shake harder and mutter, 'Get off me, you evil creature' (because she is, she SO is). Time slows. Everyone shuts up and turns to look at me. I try smiling as if there's nothing to see here and they should carry on with whatever important stuff they need to do or talk about. I even consider pointing into the distance and shouting, 'Look, over there, a lion!' But they're staring now, just as Gypsy lunges all of her filthy, hairy, wiry little body against my left leg and I'm doomed. I fall out of the patio doors on to the decking. My skirt flies up around my waist as I let out the most inelegant sound ever to grace the Quinn household, *even* counting the time Gran gagged on a piece of turkey three Christmases ago.[6] Following a short, stunned silence, everyone applauds and, worse, cheers.

I hear Mum say, 'Phones back in your pockets,' to the assembled gloaters and I'm praying she got to them before anyone captured my shame. I silently beseech Heaven to spare me having to see incriminating photographic evidence of this tragedy.

Gyp, however, is not quite finished. While I am flailing on my tummy and trying to pull my skirt down and get to my feet, she leapfrogs over me twice. Then, crossing the third time, she stands on my back and barks delightedly.

'Yip-yip-yip!'

As I get to my feet she tries to pull my knickers off, so I swat her away and she does a pathetic yeowl as if I've hurt her. I WISH. But that dog's well pleased with her day's work and prances about, barking more and showing off.

'Yip-yip-yip!'

I just know my legs now smell of her rancid breath and she'll think I smell nice and doggy-dandy, probably

6 A most strange incident and a v v weird sound.

good enough to chew on again. Even though she is not my dog, I am SO going to make sure she gets a bath this evening, which she loathes.

'Yip-yip-yip, yip-yip-yip, yip-yip-yip!'

As I get to my feet I close my eyes and silently *forbid* anyone to come and commiserate, particularly Stevie Lee Bolton. In the end Uggs takes pity[§] and he changes the subject. Though OF COURSE it involves the substantial news of the day. For a nanosecond I am actually pleased there is something more dramatic than my public humiliation to focus on.

'Congratulations,' he says to my mother.

I'm beginning to hate the sound of that word but I'd better get used to it.

Mum rubs her tummy and looks all glowing, as if everything is right in the world.

I guess I'd better get used to that too.

[§] when he's finished wiping the tears of laughter from his eyes, that is.

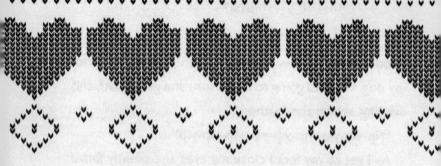

JENNIFER QUINN,
VITAL INFORMATION

Name: Jenny Q (actually Jennifer Alison Margaret Quinn). That's Jenny with a y, not Jenni with an i!

Date of Birth: 11 July 1998

Star Sign: Cancer

Hair: strawberry blonde (NOT ginger)

Eyes: blue

Height: maybe not as tall as I'd like . . .

Weight: enough

Home: Oakdale, Dublin, Ireland

School: Oakdale High School

Likes: Teen Factor X, Glee, strawberry lip gloss, singing, Stevie Lee Bolton, words, being left alone

Jennifer Quinn, Vital Information

Dislikes: her muffin top, Gypsy (next door's dog – that mutt is a menace), school uniform (it's maroon = 'nuff said), zits (natch)

Skills: singing (I make up a lot of new words to popular songs, usually with Mum – it's goofy but fun), embroidery, I'm working on my knitting too (Dixie is on a mission there)

Friends: the Gang, aka Dixie Purvis (Scorpio), Eugene 'Uggs' Nightingale (Cancerian also) . . . but not a wizard or a vampire among us. I have other mates too but the Gang are the supremo friends. (Gyp thinks she's one of the Gang – she is not.)

Family: one Gran, one Mum (Vicky), one Dad (Douglas), one brother (Dermot) – SO FAR . . .

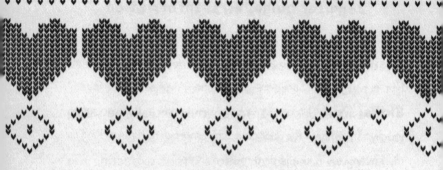

THE GODS ARE
TOYING WITH US

'Pants,' Dixie says as she enters my bedroom, where I have fled after the Horror in the kitchen.

'Tell me about it,' I agree.

'No, you're pants.'

'Er, excuse me?' I am indignant. 'There is no need for petty insults.'

'No, you idiot, *your* pants.'

Oh.

I do NOT like where this conversation may now be going. I find I preferred the petty insults. 'What about my pants?' I ask, cautiously.

'They won't do, is what.'

EEK, this means she saw them, MY KNICKERS, which means they were on show, MY KNICKERS, which means other people present saw them too, doesn't it? MY KNICKERS. Ooh, feeling a bit faint now . . .

'I wasn't expecting anyone would actually be *seeing* them,' I manage to wail.

'Have we not spoken before about expecting the unexpected?' she asks.

I'm not sure that we have but it's no time to be picky. I don't want to remember what pair I put on this morning and can only pray that it wasn't the big, comfy ones with the hearts that went pinkish because something ran in the wash.

'They're big and covered in red hearts and probably had a white background until something ran in the wash,' Dixie confirms.

'And Stevie Lee Bolton saw them?' I say in a tiny voice, hoping against hope I'm wrong.

'Oh, yes.'

'Could you tell what he thought?'

'He's hard to read, as you know, but I would say he was . . . agog.' Her mouth twitches in a suspicious way, like she's trying to hold something back.

'Though not in a good way?' I ask, clutching at straws.

'Ehhhhh, I wouldn't have thought so, no.' Then Dixie

falls back on the bed before I have a chance to throw myself melodramatically across it, as I have been planning to, and starts to laugh so hard that tears roll down her cheeks.

'They're my comfort pants!' I yell. 'I'm traumatized by life and I needed them.'

'I don't think anyone in that kitchen will ever forget them, Jen. For starters they're HUGE.'

'They're clean!'

'That's not what anyone's gonna remember about them.' She's clutching her tummy now in an agony of laughter. 'I heart pants,' she wheezes. 'Not *hot* pants but *heart* pants!'

'DIX! You are supposed to be a mate, a support, not a mocking –' I'm getting stuck – 'mocker.'

I'm really not managing this situation well. This is not my finest moment. I may never have another fine moment in my sorry life the way things are going. I really hope she snots herself from laughing, though it'll be of no satisfaction at all if I am the only one to see it . . . Unlike my huge, hearty knickers, which, we have established, the world and its mother* have seen.

* Well, my mother.

The Gods are Toying with Us

Times like this I am so glad I don't have a sister because I'd probably have to put up with this sort of treatment 24/7. At least Dixie goes home to hers every so often. What if this new baby is a girl and then I *will* have a sister and she might turn out like Dixie and I *will* have to put up with this kind of carry-on 24/7? Controversial . . .

EEEP!

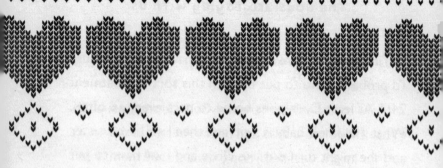

GYPSY

Dixie finally stops laughing enough to manage: 'You have big problems, *amiga*, even bigger than those pants.'

I roll me eyes. Here we go. 'Yes, I know. I was going to tell you about Mum but –'

She puts up her hand. 'I don't even mean that . . . yet.'

'Oh?' How could I possibly have a bigger problem than I already do? This does not compute . . . and I really don't want it to . . .

'Yup, maximo problemo. Jen . . .' She pauses for effect. It works. 'Your mum spread peanut butter all over her Kit Kat before she ate it.'

A horrible thought dawns upon me and I manage a hoarse croak of despair. 'She's going to eat all of my favourite things for this pregnancy.'

'Seems that way.'

'That's *so* totally serious.'

'Agreed.'

I have to know that there are good and steady supplies of top chocolate snacks and peanut butter in the house or I go into a decline. I don't have to eat them; I just need to know that they are there . . . JUST IN CASE. Of course I *do* eat them ASAP too. Why can't Mum want to eat chalk? Or firelighters? Those are proper pregnancy cravings.

'She'll be stealing for two,' Dixie says.

It's a tremendously good point, and v v worrying. That's Dixie for you: she can just cut to the crux of a problem. It's not always a comfort but it is the Way of Things. We're poring over this (devastating) revelation when there's a timid knock on the door.

'Uggs, I know that's you, but you'd better not have that mutt with you,' I shout. 'If she is, I really cannot be held responsible for my actions.'

I hear a kerfuffle and some stifled barks, so I know Gypsy is, indeed, with him.

'She wants to apologize,' he says through the door.

'She's *incapable* of remorse,' I point out, stressing the 'incapable' for good measure.

I happen to know, for an actual fact, that Gypsy lies to get her own way. OK, it's doggy lying, but lying all the same and therefore despicable. Gypsy is the same age as Uggs and me, which makes her ancient in dog years, like nearly a hundred or something.* This is probably why she is unreasonable on every point and impossible to deal with.

She's seriously messed up too and has weirdo habits. Example: Uggs says when the postman drops the mail through their letterbox she only eats the electricity bills, then goes around like a doggy zombie with a stupid grin on her mutty visog. Dixie's theory is that the glue on the envelope is made from some intensely delicious ingredient that Gypsy just cannot resist, like cats with catnip, and that's why she goes for those. It's Gyp Nip to her. Well, it's a theory, even if it's not a great one. Gypsy did nibble on a padded envelope once, but her teeth popped the bubble wrap and she got the fright of her hairy life and left well enough alone after that. I thought it was a total hoot to see her furry face trying to figure out what had just happened.

Uggs risks his life and opens the door. He's holding

* Gran has competition when they are in the same room.

That Dog in his arms so that she can't dart in (and do something awful). I start a bit of pointing and raise my voice and just as I reach a very high, shrieky shriek I notice Dermot is tramping upstairs with his mates, no doubt heading to his room to listen to loud electric-guitar music.[†] And, sure enough, they all stop a moment to see and hear me. I just know they have a vision of my huge, faded knickers and I'm now making the sound of a demented owl to go with it. (Yes, I am screeching.) Last up is Stevie Lee Bolton.

I am struck dumb then and stand with my mouth opening and closing like a stunned goldfish. My face is heating up alarmingly. At least I don't blush, ever, so that's something.

He sort of holds his head to one side and says, 'You're funny,' but I don't know if that's funny GOOD or funny BAD.

I manage to gurgle, 'Oh, you know!' with a shrug of my shoulders, as if it's all part of some brilliant plan I have to amuse people with my utter goofiness. Then

---

† That's not as bad as when they try to play electric guitar, which is TRAGIC - though Dermot is quite handy strumming on a normal guitar.

he only goes and pats bloomin' Gypsy on the head and I'm not sure if he was talking to the ruddy dog all along and not me. Why has the ground not opened up and swallowed me by now? I watch his back as he disappears into Dermot's room.

'Dix?' I squeak, like a Gyp-yip.

'Again, dunno if that was good or bad for you,' she says. 'He's nearly impossible to read.'

'You're supposed to be the sensitive one,' I point out. 'You're the self-confessed EXPERT on human beings.'

'It was good for the dog,' she says. 'Pretty sure of that.'

'Oh, that's so comforting.' My voice is dripping scorn (I hope).

'You overdo it with the word "so".'

'SO?'

She can't figure out if I am being brilliantly smart or plain sarcastic like Miss Holding,‡ our English teacher. I'm not sure myself but I won't be drawn on it.

'You went SO red,' Dixie says.

---

‡ Miss Holding lives for sarcasm, as do quite a few of the teachers at our school, though Holding is the queen bee of all the sarcastics there.

I know a) that she is using SO in a manner which is meant to be ironic and clever re our last exchange, and b) that SO cannot be true! I never, but *never*, blush. It SO wouldn't go with my hair for starters (which, as I've mentioned, is strawberry blonde, NOT ginger).

I don't dignify any of it with a spoken word but prance back to the bed and fling myself on to it like I wanted to earlier. So does Gyp. I haven't the energy to swat her off.

Uggs is standing on the spot, probably trying to make himself invisible. 'Sorry,' he mutters.

'Sorry doesn't even begin to cover it,' I assure him and add 'Eugene' for good measure. He knows that if I'm using his full and formal title he's in dire trouble.

He mutters again, 'I think you're funny, Jen. Good funny.'

I pull a pillow over my head and fantasize that if I went to sleep now everything would be back to normal when I woke up. Yes, maybe I am actually asleep and this is all a dodgy dream? *PLEASE* . . .

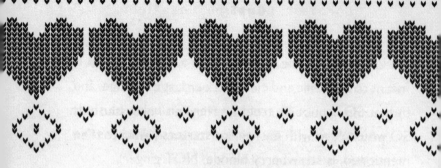

LOCATION, LOCATION, LOCATION!

When I open my eyes I am entirely and duly disappointed to see that my surroundings are the same. And Uggs still looks v sheepish, which means that my fantasy has not come true and I have definitely been humiliated on multiple levels today. He is lucky that we have been neighbours for our whole lives, or he would truly feel the wrath* of Jenny Q.

For thirteen years we have lived in Oakdale, though guess what, yep, there are no oaks any more (if there ever were to begin with) and precious little dale, whatever one of those is when it's at home. The estate is basically a grid

* Gypsy may yet experience this.

of semi-detached houses and the size of the houses is getting smaller all the time if you listen to my parents and other boring neighbour oldies. They're all obsessed with property. It's a nightmare to have to sit and listen to them when they gather over dinner and discuss:

a) what we've done with our house;
b) what they've done to theirs;
c) what they'd like to do to theirs;
d) and what mine would like to see them do to theirs.

And then vice versa on the last two items but about what mine would and should do to this house.

Of course, now that Ireland is in a recession, all anyone over twenty years of age can obsess about is houses and land and how they shouldn't have bought any when they did because nothing is worth what it used to be any more. Dermot loves teasing Mum and Dad about it all.

DERMOT: We're the ones who're gonna have to pay for it, ultimately. Isn't that right, Jen?
ME (sad and resigned, disappointed because they

25

should be ashamed of themselves): Yes, Dermot,
that's true. They should be ashamed of themselves.

It usually turns into what Dermot will dub a Classic
Sporting Moment, and about the only time we come
out on top in a family argument.

Sweet.

Uggs's parents moved into Forest Drive at the same
time as mine, when we were both bumps inside of our
mums.[†] Uggs's house is the mirror image of ours, so
everything is the same but facing the opposite way. It's
our house back-to-front. And his mum loves bright
colours in a way that's scary more than uplifting sometimes. She really *believes* in yellow above all others. It's
best to wear sunglasses visiting the Nightingales'.

Dixie lives in the next street along, Forest Walk. All
the streets have leafy names and I think the builders are
beginning to run out of ideas. Last year the latest phase
of building was Glade Vale, which just sounds like a make
of air freshener to me, or a rubbish deodorant, such as
the one Dermot uses.

† That thought is now making me feel a bit odd, a bit
dizzy, given the latest Quinn clan revelations.

26

Location, Location, Location!

My dad works in advertising and he has to think up new names for things all the time. He's forever trying out stuff on us at home. Mum says we should beware of reducing life to bite-sized chunks of words because it's way too important and huge for that. She says you can't get by on clichés and Dad usually says that clichés are simply things that are TOO TRUE. And he's not above thieving an idea either if he thinks it's good. Like, you know that campaign that went 'Poverty? Make it matter.' That was mine. Stolen. His reasoning was that I didn't need it, but he did and so did the world. He claims he was just releasing it into the community. Yeah, right. OK, I know this all makes me sound sour and cynical, but really my family are the END . . . and about to expand.

AN UNFORGIVABLE CRIME

I probably should take an interest in this pregnancy – it's not like I'll be able to avoid it. I'd get a book from the library on such matters, but that would probably start tongues wagging with all sorts of mad gossip. EEK, people might think *I'm* the one who's pregnant! This situation is a minefield.

Brian Cox took out a medical book about embarrassing diseases once, for a laugh, and everyone thought he had something awful. You can imagine the teasing he got. Obviously he has the same name as the seriously hot (though ancient) physics professor from the television, so everyone now calls our Brian 'Professor', which is meant entirely ironically but he doesn't get that (as he is a dork) and he's well pleased with the title. Mr

Ford, our science teacher, reckons physics is now way cool because of the real Professor Brian Cox being on television* and he keeps torturing us with it as a result.

Anyway, the point is that people jump to conclusions and once a whiff of a rumour is out there it grows every time someone passes it on and then we get the old 'no smoke without fire' scenario and suddenly you find yourself living in a cliché because everyone thinks it's TOO TRUE, as my dad is so fond of telling us.

'You're humming,' Dixie says, pulling me out of my daydream.

I hadn't noticed, which means I am, like, *totally* stressed. I've hummed quite a bit for singing lessons and being in the choir and so on, but when I do it and don't *realize* I'm doing it – that's a sign that Jenny Q is under siege.

'This is so totally when you should reach for your knitting needles,' Dixie says. 'It's a well-known soother of stress.'

'I'm not sure I can be trusted with a sharp stick just now,' I say.

* And not looking like the back of a bus as scientists often do.

29

'Or two,' Uggs points out nervously.

'If you ran up a tension square, you might feel better, though?' Dixie says.

Dixie may be about to go philosophical on me, using knitting as a metaphor for life, which might be fine another time but right now we have An Urgent Situation, so I call to order an impromptu meeting of the Gang, as I am clearly (and quickly) going out of my mind. I'm so far gone now I'm even willing to ignore the fact that Gypsy seems to be settling down on my pillow for her afternoon kip.

'How did we miss this?' I ask, for openers.

'WE?' Dixie raises an eyebrow. 'You'll forgive us if watching out for signs of your parents getting jiggy with each other was not top of the agenda.'

'Dixie! Show a bit of support,' I say.

I must look and sound fearsome – or deranged – because she relents. 'What has your mum done recently that's been strange?'

'Stranger than usual, you mean.'

'Well, yeah,' she says. 'It's a given that parents are strange, so I'm looking for odder than what we loosely call normal . . . normally.'

I trawl through my memories of the last few months. All I can come up with is that Mum's been sleeping a lot and that she seemed to be going to the loo more than usual. Also, she was looking a bit like she'd had too many roast dinners for a while, getting a bit chubby all round. I offer up these meagre gems.

'Classic early symptoms,' Uggs says.

How does a thirteen-year-old BOY know that? Both Dixie and I look at him like the freak he is. Which reminds me, Dixie said a while back that she thought Uggs was getting cuter, which is wrong on so many levels, not least because a) it suggests that he might have been cute to begin with, and b) he so wasn't, is not now nor ever will be. I honestly thought she'd been at the cooking sherry like her brother Kev, who is a delinquent.

There's a silence in the room – from the humans, that is; Gypsy is snoring on my pillow and probably dribbling on it too so it'll be all wet and smelly and hairy when she's done. YUCK!

I can hear the music getting cranked up in Dermot's room. He has snaffled Dad's record and CD collection because, apparently, that's brilliantly 'retro', and now he's big into a guy called Eric Clapton, so his song 'Layla' is blaring out. There's a guitar solo in there that all the lads will play air-guitar to – grossly embarrassing for all concerned, even if they don't seem to see it that way. I signal to Dixie to put on something (ANYTHING) on my stereo. Before she gets to press a button at all, I hear my mum in the distance singing along with the Clapton track and without looking I know she's bopping along to it too. She's forty-three, pregnant, dancing and singing – can she not see what's wrong with this picture? I live in a madhouse.

We spend a while in silence and it has to be said we're probably in shock. Gypsy is snoring and snuffling and chasing imaginary rabbits in her dreams.[†] Me, Dix and Uggs are staring into space, hoping a foxy plan will present itself to us.[‡]

Then there's a knock on the door and Mum is there holding a tray of lemonade and three two-finger Kit Kats – nothing for Gyp: she's not allowed chocolate or fizzy drinks for messy reasons I'd prefer not to go into

† or perhaps trying to pull my pants off me again - she likes to gloat over past victories.

‡ Well, ME, as I am the one in crisis.

just now. We accept them graciously and, when she's gone, Dixie and I let out a communal gasp.

'They weren't in the biscuit tin earlier,' I say. 'Believe me, I checked.'

Uggs is the one to give words to the unspeakable: 'She has a secret stash.'

It is so. She does. This is close to a war crime in the world of Jenny Q. It is gobsmacking villainy.

The only one with a secret stash around here is me. ME = Jennifer Alison Margaret Quinn. There'll be hard times ahead . . .

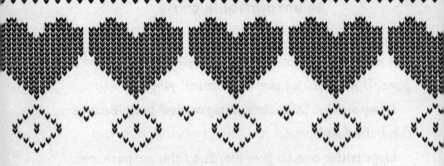

QUINN FAMILY QUIRKS

While Uggs and Dixie argue over which album should drown out the sounds of Eric Clapton, it seems the right time to take stock of the Quinn family fortunes, as clearly we are a law unto ourselves as far as normality goes. Sod's Law says that anything that can go wrong *will* go wrong. This could have been invented for us Quinns. For instance, with my dad working in advertising you'd think we'd be showered with all the latest buzzmost items, but no. By the time we get anything in our house it's *so* last year. The last time he brought something new home it was a shampoo and conditioner range that we all became allergic to and we itched like we had nits for weeks. Dad still went on to write advertisements for it as if it was harmless. Here's how it went when we quizzed him:

ME (I'll admit I was a bit on my high horse so you'll have to imagine that voice, which is high and horsey): Dad, how can you tell people to buy this stuff when it's going to bring them out in a rash?

DAD (defensive): Not everyone. Don't exaggerate, Jennifer.

ME: Oooh, *Jennifer.*

DERMOT: You lose points for being childish, Jen. (This makes me boil because he's right.)

MUM: She has a point, Doug.

DAD: Look, folks,* if I were a lawyer, I'd believe everyone was entitled to the best representation money could buy. And so, following that along, in this case I am giving them every chance of proving themselves with this product.

At least he wasn't cynical enough (on *that* occasion) to suggest he was doing it for the good of mankind (like my stolen poverty slogan).

* folks?! I didn't comment on that after the points issue raised by Dermot but I was well within my rights to.

ME (sarky): Well, anyone using this stuff will notice a difference, that's for sure.

DAD: Brilliant, Jen!

And he only went and used that! 'Try it – you'll notice the difference!' was the tag at the end of each advert. I was indignant and told him as much, in no uncertain terms. It went as follows:

ME: Dad, I'm entirely indignant that you stole yet another slogan from me.

DAD: Jen, Jen, Jen – *chillax*!† You should be proud to be making a contribution to the household with the money we've earned from it. Believe me, I'd credit you for your work if only I could, but I'm fairly sure it's illegal to have you 'working' at all because you're underage.

I give up, I really do.

Anyhow, what I mean is the Quinns are proof positive that humans underestimate the occurrence of the unexpected so much, too much. I cite this pregnancy – no

† chillax, no less; I nearly exploded.

one saw it coming.[‡] I can just HEAR everyone gossiping delightedly:

'Vic Quinn is having a baby. Imagine.' = ARGH!

But what could I have done even if I had known or guessed it was about to happen? I might have raided the cookie jar and saved all worthwhile chocolate-based confectionery, but that would have been a short-term solution to a rather longer-term problem.

I suppose I'm probably going to have to stop calling it a 'problem'. Perhaps I should refer to it as the 'surprise' and people can take that any way they please.

‡ Yes, OK, apart from the obvious people, but let's not get into that.

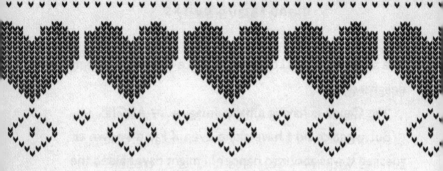

PHOTO EVIDENCE

I'm rubbish at planning ahead. And though I know we ought to be in control of ourselves, if we can't control other people, and it seems we cannot, I wonder why we bother at all. I mean if other wretches* can't be relied on to follow the basic 'please don't embarrass me, whatever about yourself' rule, what's a gal to do?

And there is more. It appears that biological warfare in the Quinn family is no new thing.

I looked up the word 'anomaly' in the dictionary a while back because I was fairly sure we had one in the family. The definition of an anomaly is 'something that deviates from what is usual or expected'. Ours lives in

* Such as PARENTS.

a flat attached to our house. It's my grandmother. She's a 'granomaly'.[†]

The major problem with women in a family is when there are women in a family. It's a similar problem for families with men. So that's families in trouble, right there, from the off. Gran (a woman) lives in what should be our garage. No one else in the estate has such an arrangement. It marks us out even further as an oddball family. Put that into the problem pipe and smoke it, as someone might say if a) there was such an item to be had and b) smoking wasn't THE most disgusting thing ever invented by humanity.[‡]

Gran is away at the moment on one of her mad painting trips, so that spares me her commentary on this whole mess. She's not one for mincing her words. Last time I fell over in front of her, she pointed and said, 'Lookit – up to her behind in legs, that one.'

Truly. Deeply. Madly. Embarrassing. I was blessed that only Mum was there, although that was bad enough, as

---

† Yup, that's pretty darned smart wordplay from Jenny Q, even if I do say so myself.

‡ Along with custard creams, but that problem biscuit is WAY too big a subject to go into here.

39

we nearly had to do the Heimlich manoeuvre on her to stop her choking on laughter and a bit of Bakewell tart that had gone down the wrong way. I dread to think what my grandmother might have come out with about the incident involving my huge, pinky pants. I gaze at my hands and think, 'At least my nail varnish matches my knickers', though colour co-ordination doesn't exactly remove the event from the annals of horrid human experience.

Gran follows the principle that if you tell everyone everything about yourself, and all about anyone you know, there is nothing else left to discover and therefore all curiosity and gossip is null and void. Which means it's v v difficult to have a secret in our house and then to try and keep it from the world and its wife.

I notice Uggs looking in alarm at something Dixie is showing him on her phone. Oh no.

The greatest and most evil of Dixie's superpowers is her ability to capture the most embarrassing moments on her phone camera. Even she can't fathom how she does it. It's like it's deep-rooted in her DNA. She's even got a photo of herself in a v compromising position with

Jason Fielding that defies all logical explanation. We never speak of it.

I turn to her. 'You've got a photo of what just happened, haven't you?'

Without a word she nods and hands over her mobile and I see the full horror. I try to be brave but I can feel tears forming, prickly and hot. I manage, 'My bum really does look big in this,' and lapse into humming again. I may need to burst into song to cure the situation. Singing comes a close second after the Kit Kat as a salve for all ills. Despite Dixie's best efforts, knitting doesn't stand a chance.

'I can't go to the Youth Club this month,' I finally say, stating the glaringly obvious. My shame is too great and further humiliation would be primed and ready for me at the hands of every single eejit there, me being the biggest eejit of all. I may never be able to have a social life ever again after this. I'll probably have to start hanging around with Delia Thomas, the oddest girl in our class if not the whole school.

'No one else has a photo except Dixie,' Uggs says.

I know he's trying to be kind and that makes me want to cry harder.

Dix understands why this is not altogether the best thing. 'That only means the story will grow in the telling,' she points out, and it sounds horribly like something my mad gran would say.

I gulp back my tears. I'm finding it difficult to breathe without giving little moans of horror and grief. Also, as mad as it is to say it, my arms and legs feel dizzy, or fuzzy somehow. It's not a pleasant sensation. My life, poor and all as it was, is over – ComparetheMockery.com is all I can look forward to henceforth. I am reluctantly cast as a tragic heroine and it doesn't feel half as good as I thought it would in any of my daydreams.[6] This is snotty and it hurts my chest and boils my heart and bungs up my eyes. It has nothing to recommend it.

[6] In those, I get to wander about in long, gossamer frocks looking gaunt but impossibly beautiful and dying of love, but rallying somehow and being utterly brave and the stuff of heartbreaking novels.

KNIT 'N' KNATTER

Dix calls the emergency meeting of the Gang to order. It's a mixture of her helping me by keeping me busy (because MY LIFE IS OVER) and the fact that she finds it v v difficult to sit still for long without 'achieving' something. It's not so much that Dixie fidgets but she's BUSY, all the time. I SO want to cry, great bawling wails, but somehow I choke them back.

There are few rules to the Gang meetings except that you have to be creating while chatting. We call it Knit 'n' Knatter. Uggs had trouble with it all initially because he's a guy and it's not very butch to knit or sew if you're a bloke, especially if you live in Oakdale. But we convinced him that it's a great thing to be able to sew a button on a shirt, for instance.* And, now, if he were to get stranded

* And it IS.

on a desert island, he'd be able to weave a pair of shoes from dried leaves . . . probably . . . or run up a fishing net from strands and fronds of, erm, trees and such. Ennyhoo, you get the idea. Thankfully he has no trouble with the chatting element of the club.

'Choose your weapons,' Dix tells us, and Uggs and I duly reach for needles and yarn.

There are always lots of projects on the go (gifts for birthdays, et cetera) so there's never any shortage of work to be dealt with. My gran finds it particularly hilarious that we knit because she thinks that's a tad old-fashioned but we have assured her that, in fact, it's so retro it's achingly HIP.

Uggs spends a lot of his meeting time rescuing balls of wool from his varmint dog, Gypsy. It is nasty to have to knit anything when she has gobbed all over it and it's therefore damp and smelly. Also, she shed hair all over a beanie that Dixie made last February (as a Valentine's gift to herself) and it was half dog, half hat in the end. Uggs said that meant it was ultra cosy and thermally insulated, but a pink hat with brown and white wiry hairs matted through, and sticking out in places, was not the effect Dix was going for.

Knit 'n' Knatter

Dixie loves knitting as much as she loves gossiping, so the meetings are heaven for her. And, because she's so much better at knitting than Uggs and I, she's 'in charge' of all of the crafty element of the meetings. It can be hilarious when she gets all philosophical, though it might be uncomfortable for me today if she tries to solve my new problems through the medium of wool.

Right now I must admit that it's therapeutic to have something distracting to do. Only trouble is my hands are shaking and I'm probably going to stab myself a few times if I'm not careful. It took me a while to get in any way good with my knit and purl stitches because I was holding my needles very awkwardly and I was pulling the wool too tight, but I've got the hang of it now. The only thing is it can feel a bit too hot dealing with all that wool during the summer heat, so lately I've been concentrating on embroidery instead.

I got some linen napkins from a charity shop and I'm making them festive for Christmas. This might seem too far ahead in summer, but, let me tell you, making stuff takes time and you have to start well in advance. Also, I have to do a lot of it away from the prying eyes of my family because these gifts are for them and the

Christmas Day surprise would be ruined if they knew what they were getting so far ahead.

I felt I was being thrifty when I got them and also recycling – it's like I'm being a recessionista AND saving the planet all at once. Each of the napkins will have a festive logo of holly and then the name of the person it's for, and a few words picked out in embroidery – kind of helpful advice. Dixie says the Gang could go into business selling embroidered or cross-stitched items with good advice on them like 'Never lick a steak knife' or 'Always tuck the shower curtain into the bath' or 'Look after number one and be careful not to step on number two'.[†] Ennyhoo, my clan napkins are customized thusly:

Mum's says STEP AWAY FROM THE KIT KAT.

Dad's is CHEW AND SWALLOW.

Gran's is DO NOT SPEAK WITH YOUR MOUTH FULL.

Dermot's is NO SLURPING.

I'm sort of zoning out over my napkins when Dix says, 'Rightyo, first rule of babies?' so I'm right back into the major issue facing the Quinn family.

'Poo?' I say.

† This one is a bit rude but it works for me.

Knit 'n' Knatter

'Nappies?' Uggs chances.

'BOOTIES!' Dix announces.

I groan. I should have guessed that Knit 'n' Knatter would have a big baby element to it from now on, whether I like it or not.

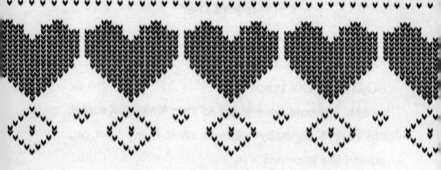

NOTEWORTHY

I love singing. Mum was so taken with this that she arranged for me to have lessons with a mad lady called Miss Langford, who wore a lot of scarves around her neck and on her head and favoured a v v red lippy and hair to match. She was actually lots of fun but I think she was usually a bit squiffy by the time I arrived. And then one day she was gone: upped and left without any warning. Gran likes to say that Miss Langford had saved enough 'running-away money' by then and left with the Raggle Taggle Gypsies(o).*

Now I concentrate on the choir. It's run by Mr Bell and he loves the sound of his own voice. He doesn't always love the sound of everyone else's. That was the

* Upsettingly, Gran likes to give her rendition of some deranged song to go with this theory.

problem with Dixie. She is v v enthusiastic when she takes on a project but she can't hold a tune. It still took Big Ears Bell twenty minutes to find who was making that 'horrible screech'.

'Is some poor creature in pain?' he asked, though none of us felt he was that concerned about whoever was suffering because he added, 'I know I am.'

He made us all belt out a hymn and he sneaked about, wincing and passing comment on all the sounds he heard. He used the word 'offensive' a lot. Dix and I were hiding up the back so we were in the final examination when she was discovered and 'cast out' as she reported it to Uggs.[†]

I actually thought I might die laughing throughout it all and Dixie really enjoys telling the story of her short career as a chorister, complete with her trademark caterwauling.

The great thing about Mr Bell, though, is that he makes sure we all take things seriously, like warming up our voices before we sing. I find that relaxing too. We don't lie around on the floor doing the breathing exercises any more though, because most of us were *so* relaxed

---

† Uggs hasn't a note at all, so he didn't even try to join up.

one day we fell asleep and he said that was 'counter-productive'. So we do our breathing and then our scales and then we sing. I think that's why I hum a lot when I'm stressed: it calms me. Also, breathing is handy for staying alive, so it's probably good to practise it too.

The best fun at choir was when a dance teacher, who uses one of the other rooms in the school for classes, came in to suggest she collaborate with Big Ears on an interpretive piece and he nearly fainted.

He clutched his chest and gasped, 'Making it up as we go along? Anarchy!'[‡]

I think if he could have said, 'Begone,' and turned her into a frog he would have: instead he settled for, 'Madam, please leave.' Then he had to have a break to gather his 'shattered nerves'.

Dixie was still in the group at the time and she does a *brilliant* re-enactment of the incident.

I'm sort of using choir practice now to prepare for singing in public solo because if I do anything at home there's nowhere to hide. The Quinns are a nosey bunch.

‡ Mr Bell likes rules.

50

ZITS

A couple of weeks later Dixie and I are lying in the sun in my back garden and she's still working on me to change my mind about not going to the Youth Club tonight, though she's wasting her breath.

Besides anything else, I have sprouted a crop of zits on my face, most of them congregating on my greasy chin, although there is also one on my forehead that would be the envy of any unicorn. I also feel a bit odd today. I can't quite pin it down but it's kind of like being poorly except that I'm not actually sick, I don't think. I ache. And I'm cranky, no doubt about that.

Sunshine will help clear the spots up, according to the Oracle beside me, but it has really got its work cut out with me today. I am Zitsville, U S of A (Unhappiest Sight of All).

I am resolved not to back down on my self-imposed exile. I am still burning with shame after my public spill at the hands of That Dog. The only comforting detail of the whole debacle is that none of the lads' girlfriends was there to witness the awful occasion.

Dermot goes out with Samantha Cooper and she's got legs that go on forever, blonde hair, blue eyes and a tan – it's like she chose all of the right ingredients out of a catalogue and, hey presto, she's gorgeous. Sam is slinky and scary. So are her friends, Danielle and Emma Louise. Together they're SamDanandEmmyLou. We call them the Slinkies. They terrify me. In fact, anyone who's not afraid of that lot is a fool.

EmmyLou definitely has the hots for Stevie Lee Bolton and makes a beeline for him anytime she can. EmmyLou and Stevie Lee . . . the sound of it makes me shake with anxiety, but, hey, it's not a million miles away from Jenny Q and Stevie Lee, although it is really.* I haven't a hope. I'm like plain Jane Eyre in love with Mr Rochester but keeping her feelings in check because they're not appropriate for someone of her station. Stevie Lee Bolton is sixteen and I am only thirteen and it's a well-known fact

* By about a million miles.

that older people are not interested in younger ones in their teenage years: an awful fact, but a fact none the less.

What do I have to offer him that she might not? Eh, *nothing*, barring some youthful enthusiasm (unwanted, see just above). Sure, I'm good with words, which is only great if you know what it is you want to say! I can sing too, but I don't picture myself serenading Stevie Lee, as that would be the act of a totes crazy person.

EmmyLou is also a true slinky – a *bona fide*[†] one. She's got long legs, perfect teeth and skin, and highlights in her hair. She also has an annoying, tinkly laugh and wears her cardigan sleeves down over her knuckles in winter and for some reason that makes everyone she meets want to do stuff for her. The Slinkies have feminine *wiles*. I wonder if this happens to all females as a matter of course. Perhaps Dixie and I will get wiles eventually, as we grow older.

The Slinkies say, 'Oh. Mo. Dhia,'[‡] all the time and clasp their French-manicured hands (no colour for them

---

† Which I think is the Latin for really real and genuine.

‡ This is Irish or Gaelic for Oh My God, which is basically the best thing to say right now.

53

this season) to their chests. Incidentally, colour is allowed in the bra department and they always, BUT ALWAYS, show a bra strap from under their tops, which are usually cropped. Sam has a bellybutton piercing and it's only a matter of time before the others go there too. And they wear matching pants,[6] I just know it.

'The reason they have longer legs than us is that they're older,' Dixie says after I complain yet again about the unfairness of the Quinn family genes. 'They've had more time to grow them.'

There's a rumour doing the rounds that Samantha also has a tattoo of a heart with her name written in it on her butt. Dixie says this is in case anything happens to her and that it's nothing more than having your dog or cat microchipped, which is funny, but there's no denying that we're both really jealous. We had dreamed of getting one each for our recent birthdays but that would have caused war and groundings at home. And the school has banned long earrings and even the eating of cheese 'n' onion crisps, so there's no way it would allow tattoos.

6 The pants match the bra, I mean, not each other. That would be too weird, even for the Slinkies.

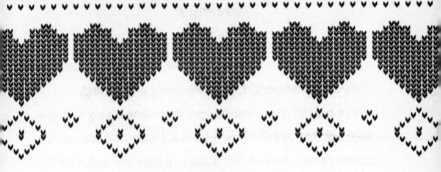

BOOBS

The Slinkies will most definitely be at the Youth Club tonight, which is another good reason not to go. The Incident of the Falling Over on the Decking and this outbreak of spots are just too much to have to deal with in public, especially against stiff competition like SamDanandEmmyLou.

I'm quite relieved even though I spent all of last week getting in and out of every scrap of clothing I possess trying to choose just the right outfit. I settled on my pale-blue denim shorts and a red-and-white halter-neck top with a navy, lurex shrug and my navy wedge sandals, but I'm now thinking it'd all have been a bit too sailor-looking and I hate themed outfits because they're only a step away from fancy dress.* It would have been asking

* I'm v v uncomfortable with fancy dress.

for trouble and having to listen to 'Ar, me hearties' and 'Shiver me timbers' type comments all evening.

I practised my make-up too, including trying to tame some glitter eyeshadow – I think I went for too dark a colour and I looked like a shiny panda for most of the day. There's sparkle on everything I own now. Then both Dix and I had accidents with fake tan, which went v v streaky, so the shorts had to be ruled out as an option. She's wearing Capri trousers tonight as a result and hoping no one looks too closely at her ankles, where all of the surplus tan seems to have gathered in an orange riot.

'You have to come,' Dix is insisting, 'for ME.'

'No, I don't.'

'What if I have to make friends with someone else and then can't get away from them ever again?'

I'll admit I don't like the sound of that. At all. 'Stay close to Uggs and you'll be fine,' I advise.

'What will you do?' she wants to know.

Good question.

I shrug and look into the distance in a profound way. I'm hoping it'll bamboozle her into leaving me alone on the subject. No such luck.

'Well?' she presses.

I give in and tell the truth. 'I'll perform surgery on a few of these bubonic boils, get into my pyjamas and eat a lot of chocolate. Maybe not in that order. Then you'll text me reports on what I'm missing.'

'It all sounds a bit wintery.'

She's right. PJs and choc need a fire to be curled up in front of. Dad might barbecue something this evening and that will have to do instead. She's giving me a squinty eye over something.

'What?'

'Are your buzooms getting bigger?'

My boobs have been slow off the mark compared with most of the others in my year, but I had been thinking they might be on the move of late.

'Yeah, maybe,' I say, and we both have a look at them till I go, 'Can we stop staring at my chesticles now or they might decide they don't like the attention and stop growing?'

So Dix holds up her newly painted nails. 'Verdict?'

Her nail varnish is a vile shade of yellow, a yellow that even Uggs's mum would baulk at. 'Epic fail.'

'It's the colour of the sun,' she insists.

'The colour of a sickly sun that has just vomited up some very runny, bad egg,' I point out. And it is.

Dix is not pleased with my verdict on her nail varnish and decides to be mean to me. 'Same yellow as –'

I hold my hand up and stop her before she says, 'Some of your zits.'

We sit in a v v awkward silence, not looking one another in the eye because we both know I have just saved our friendship because what she was about to say was true but just too personal. It's hard having a Bestest (and being one in return) because you just CANNOT be as mean to one of those as you can to your immediate family. There is a line. It must not be crossed.

Eventually she says, 'That was close,' and we both try to giggle at the near catastrophe.

SINGLE LADIES

It's seven o'clock. Dixie has left and I am speculating what will happen at the Youth Club. The Slinkies will turn up in vaguely matching outfits, as in similar styles but different colour co-ordinations. It's their version of a uniform, a bit like the Pink Ladies in that movie *Grease*. They will look fabulous. They'll hang around outside for ages so that their entrance to the club creates a buzz, which, of course, it will. In the meantime, they'll sit on the wall and laugh their tinkly laughs, and look unbearably cool and gorgeous. Everyone will want to talk to them and be part of their fabness, but everyone will be torn about going in and doing some dancing before the spotlight switches to SamDanandEmmyLou. Only a Slinky can match a Slinky.

Dad is having a beer in the garden and setting fire to

some barbecue coals. My face is throbbing with zittiness and I think I may have overdone the sunshine earlier. Instead of getting rid of the spots, it has helped them grow even bigger and now I've got a red face on me that'll peel within the week and then I'll be a flaky, hideous monstrosity.*

I sigh, resigned to the life of Jennifer Quinn. The window to the bathroom is open and I can practically hear the effort Dermot's making to get squeaky clean in the shower. He's having a major wash, as it's a hot action night for him. Then there's a lot of spraying and Dad shouts up, 'If you're using my stuff, I will hunt you down.' But he doesn't mean it.

Next is a big drama and kerfuffle because Dermot can't find his denim shirt and Mum is telling him it's exactly where she left it after she ironed it, which was on his bed. I mutter that he should have ironed it himself and Dad smiles and lifts an eyebrow. Both myself and Dermot are well able to iron our own clothes but we both avoid it unless there's money involved.

I wonder what Stevie Lee will wear and my face aches even more. I'm guessing it'll be his sexy white shirt and

* with zits.

dark jeans. If I'm not careful, I'll cry and that'll just add more red to my face.

My mobile goes and it's a text from Uggs: **U sure ur not comin?**

I don't bother to answer it. No need to because I know exactly where he has sent it from. Instead, I say loudly, 'Yes, I'm sure, Eugene.'

He looks over the fence from his side.[†] 'It'll be rubbish without you.'

Darn him for his niceness but I can't go all weak now. I sigh and do my best, cool, 'Yes, I know, but you'll just have to manage.'

'I could stay here, if you'd prefer? Not, like, with you or anything, if you don't want, but just at home.'

I swear he's going to make me bawl my eyes out if he keeps this loyalty up, so I go, 'No WAY. You are my eyes and ears out there. I NEED you at that club reporting everything!'

Dermot has stormed into the garden, still in some sort of huff about his shirt, even though he's wearing

† This is both v convenient and rules out any possibility of naked sunbathing. Thankfully, in the case of my mother, because who knows what she might do next?

it. I can smell him at a hundred paces and it's kind of overbearing. I fear he has overdone the Lynx. 'Pooh,' I say and hold my nose.

He sticks his tongue out at me and I return the look, with some crossed eyes for good measure.

'Stop it, you two,' Dad says, even though he has his back to us and hasn't seen any of this.‡ 'They didn't learn that from me, Euge,' he says, shaking his head.

Actually, I can't remember where or when most of my bad habits come from, except for biting my nails from time to time. That's directly because I saw Orla Shortall doing it at the bus stop once and I thought she looked really cool, so I gave it a go and now I'm stuck with it. I suspect I don't look nearly as cool as her, nibbling daintily, more like I'm gnawing my hand off.

And if Gran catches me mid chew she'll always say something loudly, like, 'Take that paw out of your mouth, Jennifer Quinn, or you'll end up with *hooves* instead of hands.'

Enchanté, I'm sure (not).

‡ That's parents for you: sometimes they just know.

GROWING PAINS

I'm waiting for something inevitable and Uggs delivers. 'Gypsy was wondering . . .'

'No, Uggs, I don't want or need that beast keeping me company. She's a *terrierist* and will only cause me trouble.' All true.

He actually disappears to talk to the mutt, who yips a bit as if she understands him. His face reappears to say, 'I think she feels left out too.'

'Well, take her with you, then, if you're so concerned.'

All three of us know that's not going to happen, if only because there's a No Pets policy in the hall — in fact sometimes Dixie and I threaten not to bring Uggs along under this rule, a No Pests Policy, as we like to call it.

He has another few words with Gyp and I can almost

hear her doggy sigh before the clippety-clip of her nails on the decking as she heads back into the Nightingales' house to sulk.

Uggs seems to want to stay home too. He's *lingering*.

'You're creeping me out now,' I tell him.

'Oh, right,' he says. Then he sees Dad heading inside to get food for the barbecue. 'I found out something interesting today. Apparently it's against the law to give someone a tattoo unless they're over sixteen, so we can't get ours done. Not legally, anyhow.'

This must be a great relief to him; one less fainting opportunity in the face of needles.

'We'll have to make do with transfers, so,' I say.

'Will I break the news to Dixie?'

'Do.'

There's an awkward silence.

'Don't you have somewhere to be?' I say.

'Erm, yeah.'

'Well, GO.'

Uggs gives me a miserable look, the big eejit, and I relent a little. As he slopes off I call after him, 'Those combats are SIIICK!' Which means they are in fact *brillo-pad*. He looks back over the fence and smiles. It wasn't hard to guess what trousers he was wearing: Uggs always wears his khaki combats if it's a big social occasion, and it doesn't get any bigger than the Youth Club do round these parts.

Dermot comes outside with Dad to get some money and then he disappears too, passing Mum as she brings out the bread rolls for the barbecue. She must have got a whiff of the Lynx Attack because she raises her eyebrows and smirks at me.

Then everything goes quiet. The air is really still, as if someone has deflated the garden. I'm feeling terrible and it's more than just that I'm missing the Youth Club. My head aches, my back aches, my zits throb. Most of all, I'm relieved to be here at home, which is probably wimpy beyond words.

Then I get all worried that Dixie is making friends with someone else and that this day will lead to her having a new Bestest. She must read my mind because she texts: **Slinkies on wall. Me stuck wit Delia Thomas. She v odd, 2 quiet. Plschngeur mind n get here!**

I send: **Uggs on way 2 res q u.**

Dad has poured too much fuel on the coals and he's trying to tame the barbecue flames and hug Mum at the same time, which is both dangerous and a bit EUWWW. They're discussing the recession too, so that'll make them feel like they're majorly multi-tasking.*

I get a text pic of the Slinkies from Dix. They've gone for shorts and halter-neck tops and coloured sneakers. Sam is in blue (she'll match Dermot), Dan is in white and EmmyLou is in a light green. They look great. I text back, **blurg!** and get the reply, **x actly**.

Uggs sends through a general pic of the room. I can see a sliver of Stevie's right side and he's wearing his white shirt† and his tan looks glorious. I can't see who he's talking to and that makes me jittery.

My phone goes again. From Dix: **Slinkies in Phase 2.**

This is what's happening, so — they're on the floor dancing to Beyoncé's 'Single Ladies'. I would love to tell you that it's simple line-dancing gone mad, and maybe a bit rubbish, but their routine is seriously cool. Everyone stands back from the floor and admires it and feels

---

* Apparently it's not enough just to watch TV or paint your nails when you're old.

† SEE how well I know him? YES! Destiny. I know it. Well, hope it anyhow . . .

all self-conscious afterwards about their own pathetic attempts at hitting a groove. I'm so glad I'm not there because all my zits would probably pop with embarrassment at how red and bumpy I look.

To add to my misery, I get: **OMG hairography now!** That's a super-new development. I can picture them swirling their long tresses in perfect co-ordination and the glorious applause they're getting – you'd have to be *dead* not to be moved by the Slinkies when they Turn. It. Up.

Mum comes over. 'How are you feeling?'

'Fine,' I manage, but I don't sound convinced.

She hugs me. 'You're my special girl, Jen. Always will be.'

But *how* can that be? If this new baby is a girl, I won't be unique in the family any more. And worse, I won't be the youngest either. I'm going to be a middle child and that fills me with dread, though I'm not sure why. I want to hang on to Mum for ever but I'm hot and clammy and feeling slightly dizzy.

I try to eat some of the burgers Dad has incinerated but my appetite is gone too. I'm not sure I even want chocolate or to hum, so that's pretty darn extreme.

But I bravely manage a choc-ice for dessert and it's comforting to hear the crack of the chocolate coating and feel the coolness of the ice cream slide down my throat.

I get a text pic of a tongue lurching at me and it's most unsettling. My burger and ice cream stir within me and I really hope they're not returning to the world the wrong way! I have to guess that the tongue belongs to Jason Fielding and he is making a play for Dixie. Sure enough, it's followed by another of both of them, from a very strange angle indeed. I sometimes think she really fancies him.

Uggs sends through a few more snaps. Delia Thomas seems to be hanging around the edges of his space. She looks glum but she has actually made an effort with her hair and make-up and it's not too awful. She also seems to be wearing a passable smock top. Strange. My heart gets shredded when I see Stevie Lee deep in conversation with Danielle of the Slinkies. I thought EmmyLou was the one to watch out for, but it may be that both of them want to get with him. I can only hope this causes friction in the Slinky camp – they can't have it all, surely? I want the day to end now. I've truly had enough of it.

Growing Pains

I go upstairs to my room and sit on my bed and get a weird cramp and then a funny wet feeling. I pull down my pants and there it is: I'm having my first period. I am so stunned I just sit there on the edge of my bed staring at it. It's unexpected, even though lots of girls in my class have had theirs and I knew it wouldn't be long before I joined them — I just didn't think it would be tonight. It didn't factor in my thinking. I thought I had a summertime lurgy. But this makes perfect sense. No wonder I was feeling odd.

I'm so taken aback that I don't hear the footsteps on the stairs and suddenly Dad is there in the doorway looking at me and neither of us knows what to say. I can't explain what I'm doing and I don't think he can understand what he's seeing. I must have a look of utter horror on my face because he quickly says, 'I'll get your mother,' and flees the scene.

I am mortified. He'll think I'm some sort of pervert. Then I start to cry. I am heaving with tears when Mum arrives and I can hardly string a sentence together.

'Hush, darling,' she says and kisses my head. 'It's all right.'

And I believe her that it will be. She's my mum and

she loves me and she'll look after me. We get some sanitary towels together and I climb into my big, faded knickers with the hearts on and my favourite cotton nightie[‡] and she tucks me into bed. She pulls the curtains and my room has a lovely dusky light to it now. I close my eyes and let my body relax. Suddenly everything's not quite so bad. After all, I'm sort of a woman now and I'm gonna kick some ass.

'Oh, really,' Mum says, 'ass-kicking next, is it?'

Argh, I said it aloud. And then we both start laughing till the tears come, and I think it's not so bad being Jennifer Quinn.

[‡] Like the pants, not a clothing item that I expect to be seen by anyone other than me and Mum.

LOVE HURTS

Following the Youth Club on Friday night, Dermot has a love bite on his neck! He said he'd kill me if I told anyone, or pointed it out in company, especially at Quinn HQ. He made this point v v strongly – in fact, I haven't seen him that passionate in a long time.

I don't 'get' the love-bite thing at all. The Gang tried it out once. Not on one another! No, we each gave ourselves a love bite on the back of the hand one afternoon. I didn't like it. Those suckers hurt. Why would Dermot want that sort of pain in the neck?

If Stevie Lee Bolton ever has a love bite, I will DIE (unless it's me who gives it to him . . .). Here's a song I made up about him. It's to the tune of 'My Favourite Things' from *The Sound of Music*, which is a great favourite of mine and Mum's. (I haven't sung this for her because, well, it's private . . .)

His soft leather jacket is on Stevie Bolton,
White cotton T-shirt, he plays Texas Hold Em,*
He's got brown eyes and a bright shiny smile.
He is a favourite of mine by a mile.
He might like a Slinky, which for me is no good,
I'm only thirteen and they are all well old.
He's kind to me and that's really well cool.
I wish I could be his fav'rite girl at school
When he's laughing, when he's talking,
Then my heart might burst.
Oh, Stevie Lee Bolton, I really do like you
Although I don't Stand a Chance!

Attraction to another human being is a strange thing and it doesn't seem to follow totally logical rules. For example, my mum is 'well fit' according to Gary, the dorkiest of Dermot's friends. I should point out that he's v v strange from the get-go. He likes to say 'innit'

* I'm not sure if he does play poker, like my gran does with her cronies, but I needed the rhyme . . .

a lot at the end of his sentences too, cos he saw that on TV or something. Put it this way, he didn't pick it up on his travels, as, to the best of anyone's knowledge, he has never gone anywhere and probably doesn't even have a passport.

I once heard him say he was 'biggin it up the massive, innit' and I immediately realized that neither of us understood what he had just said. Also, he's inclined to greet people with, 'High five, blood,' and then the other person has to do a high five with him and try not to laugh in his face or say something truthful like, 'My name's Marcus, not blood.'

At least he's not wearing a woolly beanie at the moment – presumably because the weather is too hot. And his jeans are up over the waistband of his underpants presently, which is an improvement. I am SO not interested in seeing his pants. My face burns again to think that he saw mine during the Kitchen Incident.[†] Ennyhoo, point is it's a bit freaky that guys think Mum's a fox in any way AT ALL – she's ancient, so it just doesn't apply. She's forty-three. And she's my *MUM*, for crying out loud!

Mind you, it's not just guys who go odd around my

---

† That memory will scorch me for ever, I am certain of it.

parents. Dix gets all giggly with my dad. She calls him 'Doug' in a funny, squeaky voice, the way the lads call Mum 'Vic' when they're feeling all cool and brave, and they sound like they've swallowed helium and have become Smurfs. Cringe-making.

And, while I'm at it, Uggs told me he was going to marry me once. He was only four at the time but it was a shock and I can only hope that he's changed his mind, cos it would just be weird, a bit like marrying your own brother, which is so totally *WRONG*. He'd also like to be called Gene but, again, that would be a Saddo Thing and it's never gonna happen on my watch, or Dixie's. Just saying.

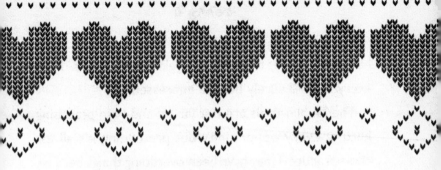

CONFESSION

OK, time for a confession: I want to try out for *Teen Factor X*. Absolutely no one in the whole wide world knows this, not even Dixie or Uggs, and believe me that's a BIG deal cos they know everything about me. Everyone says I have a great singing voice, so why not? I get goose bumps every time I think of it, just as bad as the Stevie Lee Bolton feeling, so it's serious shizz.

I watch *Teen Factor X* all the time on television and I KNOW I can sing better than most of the saddos who try out for it. But it's one of those things that would bring mockery on me if I admitted I have an ambition to be on it. Most people would just be WAITING* for me to fall on my face ... And I'm also kind of embarrassed about it, so it's my secret obsession for now – it

* WILLING me to, in fact.

has to be till I get through the preliminary rounds. Then everyone will surely be well impressed.

The Dublin trials are not far off and I am practising hard at every opportunity but pretending it's all for choir practice. I may have been overdoing things because Dad asked if I'd like to sing less loudly. According to him, he finds it hard to think when I'm warbling my numbers. Sheesh, can a girl not get a bit of encouragement round here? Would it KILL anyone to be positive about the fact that a teenager might want to sing rather than, oh, I don't know, mug old ladies?

Ennyhoo, sometimes I feel like I could burst with the tension of having such a big secret. It's a heavy burden to conceal from your nearest and dearest, I can tell you that. I also read somewhere that chocolate makes your vocal cords fat = *very* controversial for Jenny Q, if true . . .

STATIONERY

Just one more sleep until the new school year starts. And that only means one thing to Jenny Q. Some people have a thing about collecting handbags, others have a shoe habit, for me it's stationery. Going back to school means I have a *bona fide** reason for adding to my collection. I love paper and pens, notebooks, cards, Post-its (all shapes and sizes). The latter are v v handy for leaving messages for other members of the Quinn family where they are CERTAIN to see them, especially those telling Dermot he is a total eejit.† I tried sticking them directly to Gypsy to send messages to Uggs. I said I was

---

* Which means Mum or Dad will give me money to buy them without the usual arguing over what I need versus what I want.

† These are the most regular.

merely using her as one would a carrier pigeon but he was having none of it. He said it was *demeaning* to her, no less.

My desk is arranged with many sorts of folders, binders and holders. Differently coloured and decorated cylinders hold my biros and pencils, and one is devoted to my knitting needles. Lots of the pens have quirky tops with sequins and feathers and even some with bells. One whole set of pens has lights which blink when you write with them = v v pretty and v distracting. I have lots of coloured paper clips in tiny dishes, erasers in others, tacks to pin notices to my cork board above the desk.

My room is an Aladdin's cave of handy and beautiful items with which to make your mark or organize your life. If only this was as impressive to everyone as it is to me, Stevie Lee Bolton would be mine. Unfortunately, like most boys, I don't think that he is that bothered about stationery. I'm sure I would have one over any of the Slinkies if he was, as they are probably too busy being gorgeous to use a nice biro.

I'm so used to quality pens now that using a rubbish one would be like trying to write with a crayon. The only thing that has ever defeated me in this whole area is the fountain pen. I just could not get the hang of that at all, which is a shame. But it's good to have something left to conquer later on when I am a geriatric like Gran.

MONDAY, MONDAY

I didn't sleep so well last night. This happens to me a lot before a Big Day. Not like last year, though, when we were headed 'up' to Second Level and I didn't sleep AT ALL I was so wound up and nervous. I can just imagine what the Newbies are going through right now. Dix has texted **I h8 skwl** already, though I sort of know she doesn't *really*. I text back **I heart skwl** to wind her up. I follow it up with a smiley. She'll kill me for goading her.

Dad is talking to himself in the shower, asking himself questions, and this is not as unusual as you might expect. We are dealing with the Quinns, after all, so believe me when I say that strange is normal round here. I asked Dad once why he does it and he replied, 'I am the only one who knows the correct answers to those questions,' as if it was the most natural thing in the world.

Monday, Monday

There is a shard of light shining through a gap in my curtains and it has captured motes of dust and they're floating lazily around. I get out of bed and busy myself making the best of the uniform we're saddled with at Oakdale High. Who the heck thought up the colour maroon and then let the world have it – perhaps they were simply sharing the pain?

I go into the kitchen and Mum asks how I slept, so I sing her a *Sound of Music* song, to the tune of 'Edelweiss':

> 'Gypsy dog
> Some Nightingale!
> Every morning she barks lots.
> She's a mutt
> She wrecks my nut
> She sounds happy to wake me!'

Mum laughs as she puts stuff on the table for the family's breakfast, then tucks into some gherkins and a Kit Kat for her and the Bump. Strangely, the only thing this baby doesn't like is mushrooms,* which come right

* Is that strange? Probably, as I think mushrooms taste nice. Is it a sign that this kid will have Major Attitude?

81

back up into the world as quick as you can say 'get out'. And Mum doesn't like the smell of coffee any more, or red wine, which is bad luck for Dad, as they're two of his favourite things and he has to go and sit outside to have them now. Gran joins him, as she's partial to red wine and coffee too, so they have an outcasts' club going. When winter comes and it's lashing rain or snowing there'll be merry hell over the outdoor nature of the club, though they'll probably just move it into Gran's garage, or Connie's Condo, as Dad likes to call it.

Mum has managed to get the biggest jar ever (in the history of big jars) of her newly favourite pickles from the Polish shop in the shopping centre. The gherkins on her plate are all green and warty-looking. The ones in the jar are like science exhibits in a laboratory – they're suspended, lolling from side to side whenever the jar is moved. The smell of the vinegar makes me queasy and I want to gag. I *cannot* give any seal of approval to matching a gherkin with a Kit Kat craving. At BREAKFAST! It's just *wrong*!

We hear a lot of yippedy barking and I know Uggs is coming to get me, with That Dog. Gyp actually sneaked into our Geography class last year and answered all the multiple-choice questions correctly by barking at the right one as Mr Laverty read them out. Obviously a fluke but scary all the same, especially as Mr Laverty let her stay for the rest of the session and seemed genuinely inclined to take her on as a pupil. NUTS.

Gran is back from her latest painting trip,[†] so it's like feeding time at the zoo. She doesn't always join us for breakfast and often sleeps till lunchtime, as far as I can make out, but she has a sniff that today is a Big Day and so she's here to join in the mayhem. She can't resist the chance of drama and if it doesn't happen she'll make some. I remember Mum and Dad having a garden party once that was going very smoothly, everyone enjoying themselves with no problems, and Gran must have decided it was TOO smooth because she fainted into a bowl of honey-and-mustard marinade.

'Second Year, Jen,' she says now.

I grunt in a teenagerly way that I've picked up from Dermot.

[†] No prizes for guessing what we are all getting for christmas.

83

'Neither here nor there.' She sniffs at what she considers to be a fact. 'Glad I'm not young any more.' She likes to introduce a bit of gentle Age Rage into conversations.

'Glad I'm not old,' I say and bite my tongue. The WRONG thing is to engage with her, she loves a jostle. We're off!

'Old, you say.' Another sniff, for dramatic purposes. 'Oh, how *wise*, yet foolish,' she says. 'Am I to be disposable now too? Are the elderly to be got rid of?'

Everyone is supposed to feel TERRIBLE at this idea. Mum knows this and in case anyone does feel awful[‡] she steps in with, 'Now easy, ladies, it's a big day and we'll not have all that nonsense so early.'

Before Gran can pull a fast one Mum pushes her bump out and wonders aloud, 'Will one Kit Kat be enough or should I go another gherkin?'

No matter what the answer is, I'm a loser because there's already one less Kit Kat in the house, but Gran can't exactly cross a pregnant woman and make her upset. Instead we have to crunch our toast in silence,

‡ Unlikely: in the Quinn household, it's everybody for themselves.

84

aside from the toasty-crunchy sounds and the equally crunchy sound of Mum demolishing the newly invented, gack-most gherkin 'n' Kit Kat combo.

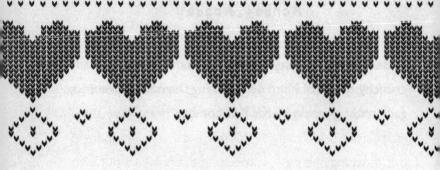

GRANDAD JACK

Dad appears in the kitchen with, 'Morning, all.'

'Douglas,' Gran says, though we all know who it is. 'What news from the shower?'

'Very interesting set of ideas from all concerned,' he tells us. 'Thank you for asking, Constance.'

They really do sit around pretending this is normal, commenting on the madness. And my gran really is called Constance.* They share a 'studio' at the end of the garden, where Gran paints her watercolours (flowery, herby and wispy landscapes, mostly) and Dad develops his hobby photographs (could be ANYTHING, and usually is). It's a shed, really, but they insist we give it its grand title, so we say 'studio' to them, MOSTLY, and 'shed' when they're not listening.

* Although it should be constant, as in nuisance.

'Dad, you were talking to yourself,' I point out.

'Well, yes, Jennifer, that is so, and thank you for that valid and, some might say, rather dull point, but allow me to assure you that Me, Myself and I were in top form this morning and have some splendid plans to put into action later.'

The whole table groans at that, then laughs.

Gypsy rushes through the door and dances around Gran. The two old ladies get on very well. Part of the reason is that Gran can indulge in long amounts of babbling on about nothing with the mutt and Gyp usually agrees with a bark or two, though that rarely interrupts Gran's flow, which is basically a monologue. She can't quite achieve that with the rest of us but it doesn't stop her torturing us at all opportunities. I think it's some sort of rule that the Oldsters have to do this, probably from age twenty-five onwards.

Gypsy and Gran are growing old disgracefully together. Sometimes Gyp stays for a sleepover in Connie's Condo. They were made for each other.

Mum offers Uggs and the Hairy Creature a chocolate-and-gherkin-based 'smackerel' and we all assume she's joking. Luckily for them they've eaten breakfast, so they're spared the latest delicacy from Quinn Cuisine. And Mum may not have been joking . . . she is pregnant, after all, and therefore a bit nutty to boot.

We all hear the front door closing and Mum asks, 'Is Dermot gone? He didn't say goodbye.'

I don't know why this surprises her – he's *sixteen*, so he's odd. He's a *teenager*, for crying out loud, it's practically his job to be moody. Yes, I know I'm one now too, but I'm new to it and it may take me some time to develop total *attitude* like Dermo has, or proper bad habits[†] and all that.

Mum phones his mobile and, sure enough, he's on his way to school. When she hangs up, she just sighs and half-smiles. 'Apparently the door closing tells us that he's gone.'

'That boy gets more like his grandfather Jack every day,' Gran says.

Grandad Jack went to sleep one night and didn't wake up the following morning. Apparently it's a 'lovely way to go'. I'm not sure about that. Dixie claims that she was once haunted by the ghost of her dead grand-

---

† Like stock-piling dirty dishes in my bedroom or overdoing things in the deodorant department.

mother, who was wafting about telling her to wash the dishes. I did ask if perhaps she had eaten too much cheese just before bed, or if her mum was going to elaborate measures to get her to do her chores. Dix has always preferred the haunting idea and insists that nothing but bribery with hard currency will be effective in getting her to do dishes.

I hardly remember Grandad Jack, so he'd probably have to re-introduce himself if he chose to haunt me. I remember he smelled of pipe smoke and had a rusty kind of laugh. The main thing about him was that he was a man of few words and Dermot seems to be going in that direction. Dad sometimes mutters that Jack had the patience of a saint, usually when Gran is giving it socks at being an eccentric.

SKWL

'Oh. My. ACTUAL. Did we, like, *actually* look like that last year?'

It really is a disturbing sight. Dixie has her right hand to her chest in horror at the hideousness of it.

'Chances are we did,' I say, more in sadness than anything else.

We're reviewing the Newbies at Oakdale High on their first day of Second Level education. Tragic. *Truly* tragic. Truly *tragic*.* They're standing around the schoolyard trying to look cool in their new uniforms. Mum is forever saying a uniform is 'a great leveller' whenever I complain about it, but looking at these guys I'm not so sure.

'Bless,' I say, shaking my head smugly and feeling quite grown up.

* And all other combos of the above.

'This year is already so much better,' says Dixie, 'because we're not them.'

Uggs and I acknowledge this fact.

'It's such a relief,' I say.

'Mind you, our uniforms might fit a bit better but they're still maroon and therefore the very actual colour of awful,' Uggs says.

'You're not wrong,' I tell him.

We still look pityingly on the First Years, like they came down in the last shower. Poor creatures in skirts way too long and too big for them because their parents think they'll be good for them to grow into. What it is, though, is mortification and I can't believe any parent could have forgotten that feeling, no matter how old they are.

'Unless they're boys, of course,' Uggs says. 'I wonder if it's unfair that you girls have the choice between skirts or trousers but us guys only have the trouser option?'

'Uggs, you guys have the skirt option too, I'm sure, it just hasn't ever been taken up by your kind.' I'm feeling all smug, having made this point, and probably have a very annoying, pleased face on me.

Dix joins me. 'Yeah, there's no rule that you can't

wear a skirt if you really want to, Uggs, least not that I've ever heard of.'

We don't continue to torture him because right then the Slinkies go by and Samantha Slinky actually says, 'Hi, Jen.'

TO ME. You could knock me over with an exclamation mark made entirely of feathers. I have been spoken to, in public, at school, like I'm *someone*. It's one thing for it to happen during the summer when we're all on holiday and normal rules don't apply, but *here*? I only manage a gurgle in return.

Uggs and Dixie are turned away now, giggling.

'Bit of dribble on your chin,' Uggs says.

'Thank you, Eugene. That is, of course, intentional,' I say.

'Of course,' they chorus.

'I dislike you both,' I say. 'Equally.'

Gary the Dork goes by, wearing a maroon beanie to match his uniform. Wherever he managed to get such a fashion faux-pas we may never know (or want to know). He goes, 'Yo!' and raises his hand and I think he may be attempting a high five with me. This all makes me gag and dribble in a very different way to the Slinky greeting. Then he does a kind of rolling walk to Uggs, like a 'homie' – in his own disturbed mind, that is – and goes, 'Dude!'

'DUD, more like,' I mutter.

'He is *so* getting worse, isn't he?' Dixie says.

'No question.'

Although Sam Slinky broke the Golden Rule of never bothering with younger people when she spoke to me, she could *maybe* be allowed off because she's going out with my brother.[†] But the Dork should know better, even if he is an idiot. There is NO WAY he should be having anything to do with us 'kids'.

The Dork spots Tommy Cook (possibly the least cool kid in the whole wide world) and rolls on over to him with, 'Tominator, ma man!' and Tommy does actually high-five him and say, 'GAZ!' That's how sad he is.

'Beyond sad,' Uggs says. 'I can't even laugh at it.'

Weirdoid Central is added to by Dixie's squeeze, Jason Fielding, who lurks into view. I see her eyes widen and take my opportunity to deflect attention as I'm still

† what they call 'mitigating circumstances' on all the television courtroom dramas.

a bit sweaty from nearly having to greet the Dork and I don't like it.

'Would that be Jason the Tongue Fielding?' I ask, as innocently as I can manage.

She wrinkles her nose, dismissively. 'That guy is *so* last Friday.'

'Yeah, right.'

'He *is*,' she squeals, then she hisses, 'SHAAA-AAAP,' as the Tongue approaches (without his trademark feature out in front of him, I'm glad to report).[‡]

'If he calls me Babe, I'll deck him,' Dixie mutters.

'BABE,' he says, the silver-tongued devil.

I wait for some violence but Dixie just, well, simpers a bit. Uggs nudges her, to provoke some action, but no go. It's like she's stuck to the spot and has lost her powers of speech – v v unusual for the Dix.

Uggs and I try to make ourselves invisible, pretending not to listen in but we *so* are.

'Wassup?' the Tongue wants to know of Dixie. 'You don't call, you don't text. I thought we had something, y'know?'

He's clearly been watching a lot of movies recently.

‡ I am thankful for small mercies.

'Oh, buzz off,' she says, and he does.

'Tough love,' I tell Uggs and I get a thump from Dixie, with a little pinch added for good measure.

'How am I the bad guy here?' I ask, rubbing my injured arm.

DAY ONE

The bell sounds and we file into the gymnasium for Assembly, lining up in our classes as our principal takes to the stage. We all call him Skinner, after *The Simpsons* character, but never to his face of course. His name is Mr Bradley. He's wearing the same grey trousers that he wore all last year but thankfully there's a dry-cleaning pin stuck to the hem of the left leg. Already there are sweat patches under the arms of his white(ish) shirt but the bit of unidentified crustiness that used to live on his striped tie is gone.

I wonder what goes through his head every morning as he scans his kingdom, and what does he make of the new geeks here in Nerdopolis. As it is, I am scanning the class lines too, desperately hoping to catch sight of Stevie Lee B. I finally spot him, sandwiched between two Slinkies (Sam and EmmyLou) and my heart does one of those uncomfortable fillippy blips that make me feel like I'm going to hit the deck if I'm not careful. And then I sink a bit because that's probably where he'll be all year, between two or more Slinkies.*

Mr Bradley smiles at us all and this will be the first and last of those we'll get from him for the year. Bradley's face doesn't suit smiling; it suits cross, stern frowning. Everything is a disappointment to him, it seems. He welcomes us all. He gives us a little lecture on the benefits of education and points out how lucky we are to have it. It all becomes YADAYADAYADA until he warns us it's best for us to see him from this angle, rather than face to face in his office. I guess he has a point.

As we file out I notice that the gym doesn't smell like cheesy old socks or trainers yet because it's our first day and it has had time over the summer to get properly aired. There's even a chance that the normally work-shy cleaners gave it a once-over during the three-month break, though it'll most likely have been only the once. I'd say they're a bunch who believe in leaving plenty of

---

* Such is the way of things, a natural law and all that.

97

germs around to make our immune systems stronger through the daily battle to combat disease.

Also, the caterers who do lunch have only just arrived, so the pong de soup du jour hasn't started to waft in yet, either, and that's a help. The canteen is next to the gym and there are days when we're vaulting the horse and the whiff of old cabbage and burger makes you want to gag. These caterers are new and they've put up a sign saying Red Rose Café and there are red-and-white plastic cloths on the tables now. Maybe the food will be an improvement on last year, which was gack beyond belief. It's a wonder any of us got out alive, actually, with the poison that was served up and paid for.[†]

Uggs was all for doing a science project on the nutritional values of what we were fed, because he was sure they were nil and we'd win a big prize at Young Scientist of the Year and also expose the villainy we had to put up with daily.

'It's a national disgrace and a threat to our youth,' he said. 'We're bound to make the news.'

As we mooch along the corridor to our new class-

---

† The final insult, according to Dix.

room I see someone has posted the details of the try-out for *Teen Factor X* on the school noticeboard and a crowd has gathered to read it. MEGA SHIZZOLA! My heart sinks, yet further than it already has.[‡] I want to tear that poster down there and then – the last thing I need is to see anyone I know at the trials and, surely, this will encourage all sorts of delusionals in Oakdale High (of whom there are many; I just hope I'm not one).

'You gonna go for that?' Dixie asks.

'Nah,' I say and hope I sound convincingly uninterested.

She shoots me a 'look' that's supposed to make me release all information to her but I keep walking without another word. It's my Big Secret and I can tell no one!

Uggs does a Dalek voice and says, 'Resistance is futile,' and I give him a good dig in the arm for that.

Both him and Dixie do a sing-songy 'Oooh' and I just want to disappear, ASAP. I make for the classroom in a hot trot.

Inside, Mike Hussy is pushing his mates around. I really don't like him. I'm not sure anyone does, actually. He's

‡ Ref: Stevie Lee stuck in a Slinky Sandwich.

99

a rough kid who likes to intimidate anyone he thinks is weaker than him. He's a bit chunkier and taller than he was three months ago before our holidays, so there's more of him to deal with now = UGH, on all levels.[6]

'Well, here they are, the GIRLS,' he says as me, Dix and Uggs appear. He makes kissy-kissy sounds intended to wind up Uggs in particular.

My hair begins to boil at the roots so maybe, just *maybe*, I am a little bit red-headed after all. I'm also still in a bit of a funk because of Stevie Lee and the Slinkies and the *Teen Factor X* stuff, so I'm not taking any more abuse.

'What's up, Mike?' I ask. 'Did you miss Eugene *that* much?'

I haven't actually accused him of fancying Euge, not exactly, not in so many words, so he's confused by that – he can't do subtlety or irony – and he's also not smart enough to think of a retort there and then. That's what makes him kind of dangerous, I think, because he broods on a thing and when he can't talk his way out of it,[§]

6 He probably has even more badness in him as a result of there being more room to store it in.

§ Which is nearly never.

he resorts to offensiveness and sometimes physical violence. However, today it shuts him up long enough for us to stake out desks on the other side of the class to him.

My hands are shaking badly and my heart is doing a funny, juddery dance in my chest. Uggs gives me a slight nod of thanks. Dix whispers, 'Good one,' though we both know Mike will be planning some sort of horrible revenge already. Delia Thomas smiles at me. She seems to know that it's not an option to do nothing in a situation like this.

I am so not looking forward to Mike's retaliation.

We sit ourselves at our single desks, with Uggs at the front, then me, Dixie, Delia Thomas, and a new girl who looks very sad to be here. Can't say I blame her.

'Why do we attract losers and oddballs?' Dix asks in a whisper, leaning forward.

'Maybe it's that thing of opposites attracting,' I say, without much conviction.

'Nice idea,' Uggs says, but his voice trails away too.

'Maybe we're about as normal as it gets round here,' I say.

'That'll have to do for now,' Dixie says, grimly.

Uggs nods. 'It's all we've got to work with.'

Yikes, we're totes screwed, so. EEEK!

HOLDING ON . . .
AND ON . . .

There is a photocopy of our timetable on each desk, as we're not trusted to take it down from a board ourselves any more. Every class copped on to how much time could be wasted doing that, so now we're faced with the done deed on the desk and getting on with things. Dixie is already colouring in the roundy bits of every *B*, *P*, *O*, *e* and *R* that she can find. She's doing multi-colour but I'll probably stick with pink, due to a lovely high-lighter I've just got.

Miss Holding sweeps in, as our first session is English. She smells lemony, as always. She has her sunglasses up on her head, as always. She greets us with, 'Another glorious year ahead,' so she's sarcastic, as always. SIGH!

I like English; it's one of my favourite subjects, along

with French and Art, because we do crafts there too. You may have thought that maybe they were my faves due to nice teachers or ones with enthusiasm for the subject (and maybe that tickles the brain, or whatever).

Well, no, not really. Think again, in fact.

Take Miss Holding,* she's a sarky witch.

'Open the windows,' she gasps. 'It stinks in here.' That'll be us that she's insulting straight off. 'Oh, would that we could learn al fresco!' She sighs.†

'We could, Miss.'

'No, we could not, Jason Fielding. None of you Second Years can be trusted to learn in any but the most stringent of circumstances.' She pauses for effect. 'And even then the jury is out.'

To look at her now, you'd think it was killing her, sapping her life's force, to impart her 'wisdom' to us, even though that's, er, her JOB. Sheesh, would it murder her altogether to start on a positive note?

There are times when I wonder if Miss Holding watches *Glee* and perhaps, therefore, thinks she's the Sue Sylvester of Oakdale High. Without being as brilliant

---

* The gang's verdict on Holding: DON'T hold on to Holding!
† I think that she'd like to live in another, earlier century.

or witty or as totally downright *baaadass* as Coach
Sylvester, NATCH. Though Holding is *quite* bad, in the
wrong, painful-in-the-butt way for us.

She does a roll call with disdain for every name on
it, then she announces we have a new pupil in the class
and asks the poor thing to stand. It's the sad girl sitting
behind Delia Thomas.

'This is Maya Walters,' she tells us.

Maya Walters is SCARLET with embarrassment as
every pair of eyes in the room stares her out.

'Maya is from England.'

Well, that does it for poor old Maya, she's *well* different from the rest of us – not only is she new but she's
bound to have a different accent from everyone else
and will stick out all the more. No wonder she looks
miserable. The one good thing for her is that she can
probably duck out of compulsory Irish‡ because of her
nationality.

By lunchtime, Maya has curled into a small ball at her
desk. Every teacher made a point of welcoming her.
They all meant well but, as any one of us could have

‡ I really like Irish but because I HAVE to do it, it doesn't
rank as my most favemost subject.

105

told them, the last thing a teenager wants is to be singled out for *anything*. Particularly if they're the new kid on the block. It's part of a general rule, along with: praise from a teacher leads to envious looks, criticism leads to jeering; and all come with mockery in tow.

We're leaving the classroom when Uggs takes the lead. 'Let's check out the new food arrangements in the canteen,' he says to Maya. 'You missed the Poison Partners from last year, so count yourself lucky.'

'They should be serving a five-to-ten stretch in jail for crimes against the youth of Dublin's suburbs,' Delia Thomas says. 'Remember the chicken tikka lasagne?'

'And the curried beetroot mash as a healthy alternative to spuds?' I say.

'We all looked like teenage vampires after a messy night on the town,' Dix remembers.

We introduce ourselves properly and make for the stairs. But we're careful not to make too much of a fuss over Maya because that would rattle her even more than the morning has already. We'd also come across as scary and maybe a bit creepy and needy too.

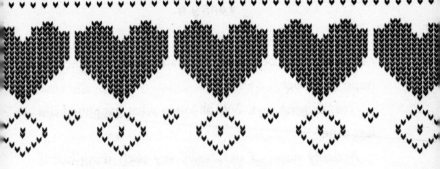

WOW

There's a snaking queue of spotty, hungry, moody school kids wanting to be fed and I think that has taken the staff a bit by surprise.

'Dear Jeebus, don't let them show their fear,' Uggs says. 'There'll be a freakin' riot if they do. Even a whiff of panic could set this lot off.'

'There's a proper salad bar,' Dix says in hushed and reverent tones. She's on her tippy toes looking over the heads of the people in front of us.

'You mean more than sliced tomatoes and iceberg lettuce?' I ask.

'I think so. I sense other *green* things, maybe cucumber and broccoli, and possibly sweetcorn. *Yellow* sweetcorn, not green.'

'Breathe calmly and deeply,' I say. 'Don't do anything

rash. Don't get too excited. And above all else, do NOT hope too much.'

'Yes,' Eugene says. 'We all know what happened the last time.'

Actually none of us knows any such thing but it sounds great, so we roll with it.

'Is she OK?' Maya Walters asks.

'Oh, yes,' I assure her. 'Thing is Dixie wouldn't dream of eating a salad for lunch; she'd be ravenous all afternoon.'

'Oh,' Maya says, but I can tell she does not understand our 'ways' just yet.

Mike Hussy bumps into me deliberately and knocks me against a table. 'Oops, sorry,' he says, not even trying to sound sincere.

I don't bother acknowledging him and make like nothing has happened. I presume this is the start of his fight back.

'Is it true your mum is up the duff?' he says. He gives a big, loud guffaw. 'Disgusting. At her age.'

My scalp is tingling and boiling again. My hand has formed a fist and I want to punch his lights out. 'We're all thrilled,' I tell him, smiling sweetly. People are watching now. I want to crawl under the table and hide for ever, to melt into the floor and never be seen again.

'The Quinns' mum is knocked up,' he says, loudly.

Out of nowhere, Stevie Lee Bolton appears behind Hussy and spills a carton of milk on him. He's a good head taller than Mike and totally fitter, so when he goes, 'Oh, man, I am so clumsy,' and starts to rub the milk in, Hussy has to put up with it and believe that it's an accident.

'Great to hear your mum's good news, Jen,' Stevie says. 'We're all thrilled.'

I think I'm going to faint. Did I dream the last few magnifeek, fantastico, unbelievabobble moments? A GOD in shining armour* has come to my rescue. Hussy will smell worse and worse throughout the afternoon as the milk goes sour in the heat but it will be worth every chokingly disgusto minute.

We watch Stevie Lee saunter away, the essence of COOL.

'Wow,' Dixie says.

'Wow,' Uggs says.

* OK, mainly maroon armour, but a gal can't quibble with this level of service!

109

'Wow,' Delia Thomas says.

'Who is *he*?' Maya Walters wants to know.

I think I may have dribbled on my blouse.

HOLS . . . PAST TENSE

I'm not sure teachers have all that much imagination. Perhaps they get bored teaching the same stuff over and over, year after year? But why (oh why) do they always give us the same assignment when we get back on our first day? So far, I have essays to write for English, Irish and French classes on various variations of 'What I Did During my Summer Holidays'. Maybe the teachers are curious about what I got up to, but I doubt it. And I SO would not be putting in what I actually did or thought or said into school homework. The world has no business knowing my business.

No, these essays will all be based on the lies I can tell using the words I have learned in any of the languages. In other words, makey-uppy stories based on the vocabularies available to me,* so they shouldn't take too long to write. And I bet you any money the same goes for the rest of my class. I base this on the fact there was a short, group groan every time a teacher announced the (same) essay as our homework. No imagination. Boring.

Now, if we were given an assignment to write our summer in mathematical terms, mine would be a sorry tale of sums not adding up. In fact, mine never add up to profit or money over. My allowance *never* stretches far enough. Good thing Mum tops up my telephone regularly as a treat. Actually, Dad does too (and sometimes even Gran),† so I'm usually contactable by phone. Hmm, yes, I know it's not out of purely generous generosity. It's so they can always be in touch and know my whereabouts – spying, in other words.

No one I know had majorly exciting hols this year. Well, Uggs was exiled to cousins in Cork for a few weeks. They put him to use on their farm and he said it was hard labour. He doesn't want to talk about cows

---

* We learned that faux is the French for false or fake, so I will be writing a faux essay!

† Gran is good for hard cash!

or sheep since, and has little enough to say about his cousins either.

'I think they thought I was not only a city slicker but also as gay as Christmas because most of my friends are girls and I dress differently to them,' he said at a Gang meeting on his return.

'Yes . . .' Dixie said, in a leading way, drawing the 'yes' out to tease him.

'I don't mind any of that, as you well know,' he said, a trifle indignant. 'I just expect a bit of accuracy and that wasn't accurate.'

He can be a tad prim sometimes, our Eugene.

'You should join us, Miss Quinn,' a man's voice tells me.

I have zoned out in Science class and I have been caught. It's a good job we weren't doing some fire-based experiment with Bunsen burners and pipettes, though that would have been exciting and I'd have been paying attention.

'Sorry, Sir,' I lie.

'Might one enquire as to where you were?'

One might, I want to say, but this other 'one' won't be telling.

113

'I was just puzzling over an earlier point,' I say.

I think Mr Ford forgets he's teaching kids a lot of the time because he really wants to be a university lecturer. He has been known to 'come to' mid lesson and ask us which year we are. Then he looks all befuddled to realize he's been telling us way advanced stuff.

If he really wants to know, I obviously bore easily and that's so easily done in his class, unless we're playing with fire and then there's always some sort of mishap. The fire brigade should be on permanent standby any time we're scheduled‡ to burn stuff in Chemistry.

Also, how has he not noticed that half the class is on the phone texting right now? *Sheesh!* And I get caught for staring into space. At least that could be counted as Physics in a way – space, you know? And time, and matter and, er, antimatter. In his favour, though it's slim, he doesn't give us an essay on our recent holidays.

I'm glad that we end the day with Art. I think it's probably my favourite subject if I had to choose just one above the rest. I like making things. I'm not the greatest

‡ Mr Ford pronounces this 'skedjooled' and he also thinks lots of stuff is 'tremenjus', so we all say that to him in his classes. He hasn't a clue that we're pulling his leg.

114

in the class at drawing or painting but I enjoy them. Miss Brown, who teaches us, has wavy, wibbly-wobbly hair and wears mad tights. Today she's got a pair on with sunflowers all over them (she must be *boiled* with the heat). But, wouldn't you know it, she tells us to do a project based on our summer holidays! Maybe it's a plot the Oakdale High teachers hatched in the staff room to drive us insane?

I find myself in a group of five walking home. There's the Gang plus Delia Thomas and the new girl, Maya. I get a mean feeling for a few moments, not wanting them to join us because I like the Gang as it is. I know this is foolish and everything changes and moves on but I don't see why we should, not now anyway. So, I'm relieved (and a little niggly, guilty bit delighted) when we turn left for our streets and they turn right to go home.

'They're OK,' Uggs says.

'Yeah,' Dixie agrees.

'But not Gang material?' I say, as if it's a question but one that doesn't need an answer. When no one answers, I have to admit that a small, childish part of me is relieved.

PAINT 'N' PATTER

I am lurching into the kitchen in search of a Kit Kat when I hear a familiar voice.

'Aha, the very woman,' Gran says.

This could be bad news for me if I am the 'very woman' she's referring to. If Gran is interested in me* she's looking for something: *fact*. I look around and discover that I am the only other person in the room, let alone the only other woman, so it must be me.

'Come down to the studio and tell me what you think of my latest paintings.'

EEK! There are no correct answers in these situations. For example, I can't say I hate something, even

---

* or anyone, for that matter.

if I do,† and I wouldn't. And if I do say I like something, I'll be stuck answering questions as to why for five and a half days or years.

'Well, I have a lot on,' I stammer, desperately searching for what.

'Is it knitting?' Gran asks.

'Yes,' I say, too quickly and without thinking it through.

'Sure, you can bring that with you and we'll have a lovely chat while you knit away.'

I'm so busted.

There's nothing for it but to go grab some knitting and proceed to the shed. On my way back through the kitchen I snag a back-up Kit Kat in case I need a sugar rush to keep my strength up during my interrogation.

Gran has a whole series of paintings propped up against the wall.

'So,' she says. 'What do you think?'

'Erm, great, yeah.' I give my knitting a look as if to say, *Jeepers I really should be getting on with this.*

Gran ignores it and asks, 'Which one do you like best?'

---

† I usually don't hate any of her stuff. I just don't know what to say about it.

I point at one of the less hazy ones and say, 'That's good . . . isn't it?' Actually, I do like the patterns in it.

'Great,' she says. (Phew for Jenny Q.) 'On my last trip we visited France and that's about Chartres Cathedral.'

'Yeah?'

'Yes, the architecture.'

I know it's going to sound totes mad but I do think it is – oh, Dear Lord, I'm being sucked into her world of nuttiness.

'Jennifer, I was thinking that you could help me with something.'

Uh-oh, what's going down now? I try not to look in any way encouraging or even to make eye contact.[‡]

'I've decided to try putting people into my work. So, I was wondering if you'd pose for me. You could sit there knitting, I'd paint you and we'd both be getting on with our projects.'

I make a kind of 'unk' sound that even I don't understand. Gran must think I'm bargaining hard because she says, 'Oh, all right, I'll pay you for your time.'

Ker-ching!

[‡] Fatal if you're trying to avoid doing something for another Quinn.

118

'Done,' I say, and settle into a comfy chair. I am nothing if not mercenary.[6]

We're each going about our business in silence then Gran starts to chuckle.

'Knitting,' she says, shaking her head in wonder. 'Never thought I'd see the day that came back into fashion.'

'Dixie says it's as good as meditation,' I tell her.

'I always hated the feel of a hand-knitted sock,' Gran says. 'Mind you, the stuff we were using was aul scratchy wool. Rope would have been better.'

For a moment I am tempted to knit her a pair of socks made of string for Christmas.

6 This means my services can be bought.

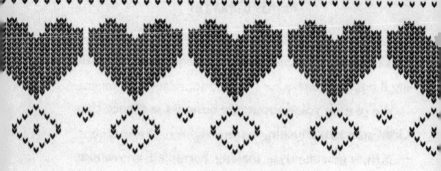

CRAFTY

A fortnight later the Gang sits around the Quinn dining table trying to plan our craft-based gifts for the rest of the year. This might not be entirely the cheapest way of doing things but it means each present is unique and I think that makes each one all the more special.

Uggs favours making bath bombs because he thinks that's slightly more macho than him knitting anything (though he is getting really good at it). He says bath bombs are somehow *scientific* and therefore more for him.

'I'm not going to make anything just yet for Bumpy Quinn,' I tell them.

I don't know why but I don't want to attract too much attention to the new baby in case it's bad luck. He or she needs to get out into the world before I go there on the gifts scene. I'm also sort of getting used to the idea that he or she will be with us for the New Year and not for Christmas, so no gift need apply, and I am maybe, *maybe* getting a tad excited about it all too.[*]

What's really getting to me right at the moment, though, is that the trials for *Teen Factor X* are now only a few weeks away and I haven't decided what to sing. Not being able to ask advice from the Gang because I haven't told them is eating me up.

I'm just so afraid someone will say, 'Don't be daft,' because it probably is a really stupid idea. Uggs and Dixie are my Bestests but they would have ammunition for teasing me till Doomsday if they knew I was trying out for it. And if I tell one of the Gang, I have to tell both.

The only time this wasn't an issue was when I got my period. I told Dixie about that but not Uggs. It would be way too embarrassing for him and me to have to discuss *that* kind of personal thing. I know he won't mind and in time he'll guess that I've started menstruating,[†] like when we're in our twenties or so, which is aeons away.

[*] MAYBE!
[†] What a horrid word! And why does it have MEN in there and not WOMEN???

I don't know if there's anyone in my family I could trust not to blab either. Probably not. Mum would tell Dad, natch. Gran can't keep anything to herself, not if there's torture value in it and she'd find plenty in this. I don't have a sister (yet . . .). And Dermot wouldn't be interested, though he would be only too delighted to have an opportunity to tease and embarrass me about a whole new thing. I'm humming a lot.

'Why are you humming so much?' Dixie wants to know. 'What's the matter?' She and I are knitting away, so I should be all chillaxed according to Dixie's philosophy.

I have to be quicker than a very quick (knit) wit here. 'I'm going to be a middle child and therefore forgotten,' I say, and I am well pleased with my ruse. It's a *deflection*. Then I top it with a deadly fine change of subject. 'Why are you not speaking to Jason the Tongue any more?'

'Well . . . he posted a picture of me on Facebook.'

'And that was bad for why?'

Dix puts down her knitting needles. 'It's entirely unflattering *and* from a very strange angle, all of which would have been fine because I was unrecognizable but then the oaf only went and tagged me in it so everyone knows it's me.'

crafty

This is indeed unacceptable behaviour. And it needs to be investigated urgently or, as the French might say, 'toot sweet'. I fire up the laptop and log in and sure enough there's a v v horreeblah photo of Dixie for all to see.

'Eeep,' I say.

I understand completely. Dad is forever taking photographs of us and then framing them around the house in full view of any visitor to JQ HQ. If it's true that a little bit of your soul is robbed every time your photo is taken, then I am probably close to being an empty husk by now, courtesy of my father. And that's before we even get to the embarrassment factor, which is to the power of *for ever*. Thankfully, after some harsh words (and some foot stamping), Dad agreed to keep all the portraits of us naked, or in silly clothes and with awful haircuts, in our parents' bedroom. After all, they are the only ones who could possibly 'enjoy' looking at them.

'There is nothing else for it; you'll have to put up one of him being the Tongue.'

'Correcto,' Uggs says. 'It'll balance out the awfulness.'

Dixie looks unsure.

123

'You've got one from the Youth Club,' I remind her.

'It's the only way, Dix,' Uggs tells her.

'It'll be *karma*,' I say. 'Coming back to bite him on the behind.'

Dixie usually likes the idea of justice in the world, so I think she'll like this too. Besides, it's hardly much of a payback – all we're doing is replying in a language that the Tongue understands. He posted a photo of Dixie that is at best *odd* and at worst *mortifying*, he didn't ask her permission and then he named names = *nah*-ah-*ah*!

'If this backfires, in ANY way AT ALL, you are both dead,' she warns.

The stakes are high. We both nod encouragingly. Within minutes the photo is posted and Jason Fielding tagged. All is well in the world, for another few hours at least. And I have avoided speaking about *Teen Factor X*. Phew.

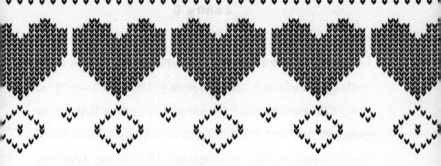

LISTS

I love making lists and I especially love crossing things out on those lists when they're done. I select a blue pen with a mauve feathered top from my newly upgraded and expanded stationery selection and write down the knitted items I intend to make in my make-and-do notebook. I'll probably cross out 'done' items in red pen when the time comes, because that will be final and dramatic, and *achieved*.

In order of difficultness:

1. GRAN = fingerless mittens*
2. DAD = skinny tie
3. MUM = cowl
4. DERMOT = beanie hat

* I'm absolutely not advanced enough in knitting technique yet to tackle fingers.

Dix tells me the trick with the mittens is to knit a flat rectangle and then make it into a 'tube' by sewing up the side, leaving one hole for the thumb and the four other fingers just stick out the top. Foxy tip and proof that I'm still in the kindergarten of knitting, whereas Dix is, I think, a graduate.

Uggs is going to make stuff from found objects, or recycle jars and such like. We're all agreed that jam jars would make nice hanging nightlight holders and coloured jars would be even more ideal. We are officially on the hunt for Interesting Items now.

'And saving the planet,' Dix says.

It's a lot to take on.

'Where's your list?' I ask her.

'I'm still at the planning stage in my head,' she says. 'Preparation is the most important part of the process, you know.'

That's a bit preachy, I think, and she's avoiding work, but I let it go. I don't want her getting uppity and maybe turning the spotlight on me because then I might spill the beans about my *Teen Factor X* plan, which would be v v *not good*. So, with superhuman effort, I cease humming too.

Lists

'I'm going to knit Gypsy a little sweater,' Uggs says.

'Tremenjus,' as Mr Ford would say, though I really don't see what Uggs sees in that dog or why he would bother making her something.

'We'll need to go to town to get supplies for our various gift efforts,' I say.

'Excellent idea,' Dixie agrees.

'You don't need to come along,' I point out. 'You have no plans and therefore no shopping list.'

'It's shopping, no matter who it's for,' she squeals. 'I can't miss that! Besides, you need me. I will be a discerning eye, without emotion or bias, when it comes to making important decisions.'

Both Uggs and I give some 'hmmms' but we all know we don't mean them.

'I may be inspired by the day,' she says. 'You can't deny me that chance. It would be *thwarting* my creativity.'

She has me with 'thwarting', because she knows the power of a good word over me. Uggs is nodding because he understands that too and he enjoys a good word, well used, himself, it must be said. Then Dixie nails it with '*stifling me*'. She's good, very good . . . oh yes . . .

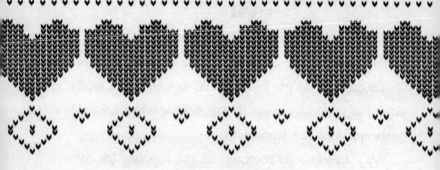

GRUBBY

The radio is playing 'Crazy in Love' and Dixie shouts, 'Choon!' and turns it up. We all love a bit of Beyoncé. My mind wanders to Stevie Lee Bolton, as it is inclined to do. This always makes me hot and bothered and today is no exception. It strikes me that being in love must be a bit like being afraid, because it seems to have all the same symptoms. Then again, I don't really *know* Stevie Lee that well, so could I really be in *lurve*? So I'm guessing that Stevie Lee does something chemical to me and therefore it could be merely a crush/lust on my part. I'm not sure he notices much about me unless I fall over and show my pants,* so it's hardly what we could call a relationship . . . or *love* . . .

Suddenly everything's all blown apart by the sound of cannons firing. Gypsy starts barking somewhere in

---

* Tick, done that, should've bought the T-shirt.

the distance. There's also, simultaneously, a lot of loud music coming from Gran's garage. It sounds like there's a battle going on in there.

'OK, I'm going to have to ask two questions,' Dixie says, in a resigned tone. 'Question one: where is your mum?' She waits for an answer.

'Yoga.' Though how Mum can be bendy with a bump is beyond me. She says it's about relaxation but it's still all bendy stuff as far as I can make out. Bet it looks v v strange. And apparently it's a class for pregnant women, so they'll all be bendifying themselves[†] with bumps getting in the way of the bendiness.

'Question two: what in the name of Beelzebub is that noise?'

The din is bad news for the Quinns. Gran is playing the *1812 Overture* and not in honour of the Proms or anything like it.

'Gran's gearing up to cook,' I say. 'That's her version of that thing the New Zealand rugby players do before a match.'

'The haka?' Uggs says.

'Yeah. She's psyching herself up.'

---

† A room full of bendy, bumpy women = shiversome sight.

129

'Whoa,' Uggs says.

The whole house now feels like it's shaking: a 6.5 on the Richter scale.

'Is this a regular thing now?' Dixie asks.

'No, she doesn't do it if she's just cooking for herself, it's only when she's in charge of the main family meal.' I shrug as if to say, *Whaddayagonnado?*

Truth is Gran can't cook. The Quinn Clan would be better off if I knitted us a meal; that would be tastier, more nutritious and easier on the eye and tummy, no matter what I knitted it with. Even an embroidered tomato would be better than whatever Gran might do to the real thing. She has been known to merely wash fruit and yet still destroy it or make it inedible.[‡] It's an astonishing skill.

Gran bursts into the kitchen on her mission, Gyp yapping at her heels. They are both in high good form.

'Aha! The youth of today, scheming and scamming I hope?'

We nod guiltily, although we were scheming for GOOD, which is actually more than can be said for her

‡ She could probably have got a job with the caterers in our school last year, the Professional Poisoners.

and what she's about to do to an entire family — a generation could be wiped out!

'I have decided to be recession-busting and make tonight's supper from whatever ingredients are available in the cupboards and fridge,' she announces.

Uh-oh – last time she tried this she made a loaf of some sort which tasted like the wooden spice rack had been soaked in water and heated up in the oven.[6] She *called* it a meatloaf but it was, in fact, a crime against humanity.

'I think there are some pizzas in the freezer,' I yelp, helpfully.

'Why the fried egg[§] would we want them? No good in them at all,' she declares. 'They're snacks for watching TV, not a meal.'

'Should we not wait for Mum? She might have something planned for us?' I'm sure I sound desperate, panicked.

'Nope, she asked me to do it.'

Mum must be well annoyed with us for something we did, or perhaps the baby has eaten her brain, which has

---

6 Full of roughage, though: the Quinns were 'regular' for a week after that one.

§ Gran tries not to swear around us younger folk.

been known to happen to pregnant women for the nine-month term before the child emerges into the world.

I decide to spring into action, which is not natural or acceptable for my kind: I am a teenager so my default position is lying about moodily, complaining about my circumstances or sleeping (like a cat). This, however, could be a matter of life and/or death.

'Domestic Drama in motion,' Dixie whispers.

Gran is rooting through the vegetable rack. 'I could make a big stir fry,' she says.

I look over and see that the ingredients for this would be turnip, rhubarb and cabbage. Yumtastic, *not*!

'Mushroom and baked-bean omelettes?' she wonders. 'Or mango and chickpea soup?'

Uggs is paying *way* too much attention to his bath-bomb formula now, which means he is trying not to laugh.

I shout up the stairs: 'Dermot, Gran is planning supper,' and quicker than 'Stop you right there!' he's here in the kitchen.

'Steady on, Gran,' he says, leading her to a chair. 'I forgot to tell you that Mum said for you to relax and Jen and I can look after the meal.'

'Yes,' I say. 'It'll be a great, em, team-building event for us.'

'Ah! I'll have a glass of wine so,' Gran says.

I look at Dermot conspiratorially. We intend her to have a few if it will save her from murdering us, or from a charge of manslaughter, or clanslaughter, or whatever a court of law might throw at her.

Dixie, Gyp and Uggs take their leave, smirking (Gyp) and wondering in whispers to me if we'll make it through the night (my more human friends).

Dermot and I take the pizzas from the freezer and heat them, adding some extra cheese and tomatoes – a foxy Quinn trick to jucify and tastify them even further. We serve them with a bag of salad found in the fridge for some fibre and greenery, followed by fruit with a scoop of ice cream for afters and 'Shallakazam!' supper is sorted and the family saved.

Mum and Dad arrive home just as the pizzas are ready, raising an eyebrow or four at the sight of their children in the kitchen. I admit it is a rare sight in the Quinn household but they could at least try to keep their mouths from hanging open.

'Emergency,' I say, nodding my head towards Gran.

133

'*1812 Overture?*' questions Dad.

Dermot holds up the turnip and rhubarb that he's returning to the fridge, and no further explanation is required.

Gran is slightly giddy by the time we get to dessert and smiling broadly at the world. She even sings a short medley of songs, which is usual when she's had a glass or two of vino because she can never remember all the words to any *one* song. Then she tries to get us to do some party pieces but Mum eventually convinces her to go watch television in her own place. Dad looks like he might have a heart attack trying not to laugh out loud in front of either Mum or Gran.

For once, I wouldn't have minded a sing-song, as I need to practise in front of people** and choose a song for *Teen Factor X*. A made-up song on the delights of the day performed alone, or for my mum, is one thing, but a performance number is altogether another. I also don't want to make the mistake of doing anything too recent or too popular because everyone else will surely be doing that and I'd prefer not to be like the rest of the herd. Perhaps there will be something in Mum and

** without them knowing, obvs.

134

Grubby

Dad's ancient CD collection that will make the judges think I am 'classic' and other such star-quality buzzwords.

Thinking about my song choice makes me feel slightly sweaty, and a little bit guilty. My pizza does a jump inside of me as my nerves kick in again. I must be insane thinking I can do this. I wish I could tell the Gang but, in this case, a problem shared might be a problem trebled.

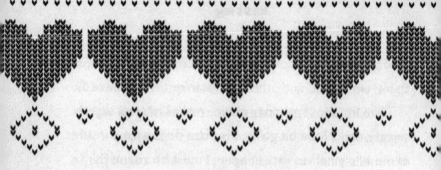

KISSING

Later that night I finally break down, overwhelmed by curiosity, and text to ask Dixie what kissing Jason Fielding was like. I figure texting should save us both any unnecessary embarrassment, even though we are Besties. She replies immediately: **wet**.

Frankly that doesn't fill me with desire to kiss guys, if it's gonna be all slobbery. I might as well kiss a frog for the sliminess involved. And I'm not sure I want someone else's tongue in my mouth. But then I imagine what it would be like to kiss Stevie Lee and it's not at all spitty; it's gentle and romantic. His lips are soft and caress mine* and if he does want to introduce tongue action I just know it will be lovely too and not at all like Jason Fielding's.

* For ages!

Kissing

Actually, now that I think of it, I can't imagine what Dixie was thinking of, letting the Tongue snog her. Did she like it? Does my Bestest like spittiness? It's a worrying thought. Stevie Lee Bolton does not slobber and he smells nice.[†] He also *appears* to wash regularly, so that's a definite plus. I think he holds my face with both his hands when he's kissing me too, like in the movies.

It makes me agitated to think of all this romance because it may be entirely hopeless. It IS hopeless, unthinkable. The age gap between us is too huge – three whole years. I haven't a hope, really. I am resigned to the fact that despair is all that I can look forward to when it comes to Stevie Lee and me.

If I die without kissing him, I'll DIE!

[†] I'm not sure I've ever actually noticed what he smells like, but surely it's as good as he looks?

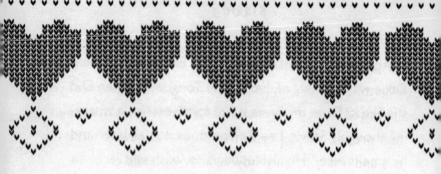

LOL

I catch a glimpse of Stevie Lee Bolton as I'm crossing the schoolyard in the morning with Uggs and Dixie. He nearly makes the Oakdale uniform work. I find myself laughing too loudly at something Dixie says in the hope that he'll notice us, look over, *glance* our way.* It's a split-second of madness and I sound like a deranged hyena.

'Steady on, Jen,' Dixie says. 'It wasn't that funny.' She pauses and considers. 'Or was it? Yes, maybe it was.' She is now delighted. 'Watch this space, folks, I may be having one of my brilliant days.'

'Look out, day,' Uggs says and gets a casual thump for his pains.

Even though SLB didn't look our way, I have a little

* I am hoping desperately for another canteen 'moment'.

flutter in my heart that he's in the building. This crush is getting out of control, but then again I think that's supposed to be the general nature of crushes. It's my first proper one on a real person, so I'm new to all of this and not quite sure how exactly it should go.

In our classroom Mike Hussy is running amok. He's tipping desks enough to make books and pens tumble to the floor, then pogo-ing around and shouting rude songs and insults and banging into people.

'That jerk's got issues,' Dixie says.

'Well, good morning, LADIES,' he says to us, eyeballing Uggs.

'Takes one to know one,' I tell him. I know it's *super* lame but it's a reflex retort and all I have at this early hour.

Mr Foley arrives for History and the class settles. Mr Foley is v v proud of being Irish and that's good. But as a History teacher I think he stresses the Irish stuff a bit too much, all the trouble in the past particularly. Ireland is more than that now and we need to move on, and being Irish means a lot more than it did when he was growing up in the 1960s (or whenever, last century).

I look around the class and there are all colours of

skin to be seen – white, black, brown, freckled. I remember once at primary school a teacher brought in things that weren't all they appeared to be, to show us not to judge by appearances alone. She had a passionfruit with her and we all said it looked like an old, dried poo, but then she cut it open and inside it was all juicy and delicious.

Mr Foley is telling us all about how much work he is going to pile on to us this year, and so I start to zone out. The Gang has phones on silent but we can sneak looks at texts as they come in. Mine lights up, it's from Uggs: **MIKE HUSSY IS AN (_I_)**. I nearly choke on my snort of laughter – we have a new emoticon and it's for arse = way cool and BAAAD(ass!). Dixie follows up with: **HE'S A (__I__)** = even better, a FAT ASS! I don't know if I'll be able to concentrate after such brilliance. All I can manage is to congratulate them both with: **LOL!**

BULLY 4 YOU

'Why can't people get on with one another?' I ask Mum when I get home that afternoon. 'Why do some of them have to be mean to other people?'

She has a big sleepy head on her. She's rubbing her bump and I think the critter is moving about a lot inside.

'Is this something to do with school?' she asks.

'Sort of.'

'Well, not every group that's put together is going to get on totally as a whole.'

'Like being in a family,' I say, and she smirks as if I've said something funny. But I didn't mean to. It *is* like being in a family, surely? I mean to say, would I like Dermot if he wasn't my brother? Maybe not. I probably wouldn't even get to know him. I'm not sure I do know him, even though he is my brother. The only time I spend with him any more, really, is if we go on a family holiday.

'Having to deal with different people can be a lesson in compromise,' she says. 'For the good of the group.'

'But is that not just letting people get away with bad behaviour?'

She looks at me seriously. 'Is there a problem at school, Jenny?'

I don't know if I should be talking about this to an adult. No one likes a snitch. But she's my MUM. She's here to help, always, that's the deal with mums. And dads too, for that matter.*

'One of the boys is being mean to everyone, but especially Uggs. He says he doesn't mind but I think he does. I know I do. I don't like it, *at all*, but if we say anything, like, *official*, we might make things worse. Even sticking up for yourself gets you more grief from him.'

'This boy is probably very unhappy.'

Not my problem, I want to say, he shouldn't take that out on other people, but I shrug instead.

'Why don't you leave it until Friday and if it has got any worse we'll come up with a plan.'

I nod, though it's hardly a RESULT.

---

* Brothers and sisters maybe not so much.

'Kit Kat from the fridge?' she asks.

Does the bear poo in the wood?

'Er, *yeah.*'

I pass on the offer of pickles.

It feels good to share, even if part of the sharing has involved my favourite snack. For a mad moment I want to tell Mum about *Teen Factor X* but I am so afraid of ridicule or even a smile at the idea of it that my self-confidence vanishes and I say nothing.

I'm reading a book set in London in Victorian times and it's full of adventures and smells and sounds and excitement and murders. It makes me feel nothing happens in my life. Is that a bad thing? IS it OK to live a dull life? Will I ever make my mark on the world? And should I? MUST I? What have I got to offer? I'm probably wasting lots of opportunities to use my talents, whatever they are. It makes me feel like I HAVE to go for *Teen Factor X*, rather than just wanting to. It makes me all jittery again, so even the Kit Kat has trouble settling me.

I decide to do something practical,[†] so I go up to my room and start knitting a skinny tie for Dad with some

---

† This does not include homework, obvs!

143

green cotton that I have in my bag of yarns. This is something REAL and not a dream, like *Teen Factor X*. I can't help but imagine what it would be like to win. I'm really not certain that showbiz is the life for me, especially now, at my age. The whole thing still fills me with fear. I guess I wonder if I'm in any way good enough at singing and I'm terrified in case I'm not. I wish I could juggle brilliantly and then that could be my act for the show and it would have novelty value and everything the judges and the public seem to want.

I try to lose myself in the knitting, as I have been told is possible by my Lifestyle Guru (Dixie). Dix is actually a good teacher, and strict too. She's slightly less sarcastic than the staff at Oakdale High but maybe that's an age thing and she'll grow more cynical as she gets older? She insists that the Knit 'n' Knatterers double-check the instructions that come on the yarn – that way you'll avoid a disaster later on when you might find your sleeves would suit an octopus's arms rather than your own or that the sweater you knit is in fact a maxi-length dress.

I'm still working with the two most basic stitches = KNIT and PURL. Dix says that if those are the only two

 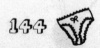

I ever master I'll still be able to make lots, and not just plain things.‡

As I'm knitting and purling, I start to warble a tune, then I let rip altogether. My bedroom window is open so anyone might hear but I don't mind. Then Gypsy starts yowling in the Nightingales' garden and, believe me, she's no help. Everyone says she's singing along when she does this but I doubt that v v much.⁶ Her doggy yodelling is so bad I actually start to laugh and cannot finish my song. I even drop some stitches. She is a proper menace.

‡ I use bamboo knitting needles, by the way, because they feel lovely and don't make v loud and annoying clickety-clackety noises.

6 The mutt is sabotage on four legs and mega-unmusical and v loud, the opposite of harmony.

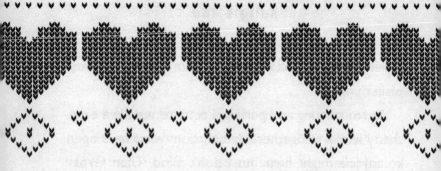

THE BUS OF EMBARRASSMENT

Friday is always the best night of the week, knowing there is no school the next day. After loads of list-writing the Gang has a shopping trip planned this weekend, which will be large amounts of fun. Before I go to bed I hide my savings tin under it.* I had to start the sneakiness because Mum was forever 'borrowing'† money. She says, in her defence, that she always puts it back, but the first time I noticed some missing I went into a proper strop about having a thief in the house. Quite rightly, I felt, but then *I* ended up having to apologize for throwing a hissy fit, even though I didn't think I had anything to apologize for. Now I move the hiding place regularly so that no one

* Its current location.

† Erm, STEALING.

is even tempted to steal – I mean *borrow* – from me any more.

I have a good stash at the moment because I've been thrifty with my allowance and Mum and Dad pay us for special jobs around the house. I've been volunteering for lots of those, like washing the car or weeding in the garden. And Gran hates vacuuming, so she's usually good for a few euros for that. Oh, and dusting: that is one *boring* activity! Of course I am a paid artist's model too, from time to time, even if it is Gran who's the 'artist'.

The next morning, the Gang get the bus and sit upstairs but not right at the front because we might look like total kids if we did and we're teens now and have had to give up some of the fun childish things. I nearly lose my breath when Stevie Lee gets on a few stops after us and comes upstairs too. He's with some of the lads and doesn't bother to say hello. Well, actually we don't look around because we're being cool, so they'd have to be really UNcool if they were to try to get our attention, which they SO don't need to do because they're, like, SIXTEEN and needn't bother with us. They sit in the long back seat and I just know my neck is bright red from him being close by, which he will SO see because my hair is in a ponytail. I hope I have no spots back there, either, flashing up even redder than my sweaty, red neck.‡

I try to open the window above me to create a breeze but all that happens is that I catch my hand in it and then, when it's ajar, a branch of a tree whips in through the space and thwacks me. I have to pretend it's no big deal or everyone will be looking at me and if I draw attention to myself I just KNOW someone will remember the pants incident from the summer and mention it and I'll be megamorto.

I'm stinging from the window, the tree and major embarrassment now. Why do I have to be so clumsy? I feel slightly sick at the thought of falling off the stage during my *Teen Factor X* tryout. Why did I even THINK of that? With the Quinn genes lurking in my body, now it's almost guaranteed to happen. I glance guiltily at Uggs and Dix but decide that this is even more reason not to tell anyone so they don't insist on coming along to witness my humiliation.

‡ I bet some more will sprout by the time we get to the city centre because of my anxiety.

The Bus of Embarrassment

You'd have thought it would be better when the bus stops for us to get off but that's when it's worst, if you ask me. I delay as long as possible so that anyone cool from Oakdale wanting our stop too might be ahead of us and have gone on to the mean streets of Dublin without noticing us[6] too much.

I let Uggs and Dixie get a head start, but all that happens is that I delay TOO long and the bus has started to drive off so I have to come crashing down the stairs in a v v awkward way, shouting, 'Wait, wait, this is my stop!'

Like a lunatic.

Most inelegant.

Stevie Lee is right outside the bus doors as they fly open (*mega* ARGH!) and he helps to steady me when I tumble on to the footpath. He does actually look concerned, but also like he's gonna burst out laughing. I brush him off with, 'I'm fine, really, just couldn't find something from my bag under the seat and then I lost my footing on the steps,' which is (Way) Too Much Information.

He goes, 'You're such a funny little thing.'

6 I.e. ME and my amazing clumsiness!

149

Er, WHAT??? This is not good. A 'funny, little THING'? Exsqueeze me?

When he is safely out of earshot further up the street with his pals, Dixie says, 'Way to go, lady!'

She is the definition of irony§ with this. 'You made an *impact*,' she continues, for good measure.

Uggs says, 'Jen, there is never a dull moment with you around.' And there's no irony there: he means it.

I am *scarlet*.

We cool me down with an ice cream** and I find the will to carry on, JUST.

§ = the opposite of what she is saying.

** A Solero for its refreshing, fruity taste.

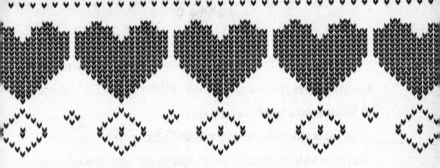

DOWN TOWN

First up, Uggs needs his bath-bomb ingredients to test out before making his main Christmas batch. Many of these can actually be bought in the baking aisle of the ordinary supermarket, so he's already got most of what he needs, but citric acid costs a lot for small amounts there, so we head to an Asian shop to get it. Uggs said he asked about it in the local Oakdale Pharmacy and they wondered was he on drugs and he doesn't know why (probably best not to either!).

We buy what he needs and have to drag Dixie away from a *v v* vibrant henna, because one 'scientific' experiment is enough to be going on with and if she ends up with orange hair we'll all be in trouble. We nip into a health shop and Uggs gets grapefruit oil to make the bombs nice and smelly. To be extra thrifty we'll root around our bathrooms for other essential oils and donate some portion of those to him – I call it a spirit of 'waste not, want not'.

Dixie is no help on our quest because she just wants to clothes shop, even though she hasn't got any money. She keeps wandering off or distracting us. We eventually give in and agree to visit Primark and River Island with her but, by then, the damage is done and all she wants is style checking, so we leave her to that and agree to meet her on O'Connell Street an hour later. So much for her getting all inspired to create gifts for others. Uggs is loyally coming to the wool shop but I feel a bit like I'm being stalked as he trails around after me.

'I have to think about Gypsy's little coat,' he says, and I remember he has vowed to knit her one. Sometimes, though he is one of my Besties, I think he is odd and that mutt even odder.

I spend a long time trying to persuade myself to stay within a strict budget on yarns but I fall in love with a deep purple colour in a cashmere mix and, even though it'll have to be knitted on smallish needles and therefore take longer, I know I have to have it for Gran's fingerless gloves.* I get a ball of black double-knit cotton and a lime green for Dermot's hat, which is now going to have stripes as a result, and there are some balls of chunky light purple wool in the bargain basket for Mum's cowl, along with a bobbly kind of mix that might look good as a fringing for that.†

I should be glowing that I have done so well with my purchases but everywhere we go I see posters for the *Teen Factor X* auditions. The whole world will turn up and I won't have a chance of progressing. It's getting me down. Then it occurs to me that it's all over Facebook too, so it's not like everyone doesn't know about it; the posters are just like tinsel on the readily available information. AND, while I'm at it, there have been adverts for it on television and radio. I really am densely stupid sometimes.

Uggs stops me just before I get mown down by a taxi as I blindly cross a road. The angry, blaring horn brings me back to the Dublin street he has hauled me back on to.

'What's up, Jen?' he asks. 'You are so not *you* right now.'

Oh no. There is something so trusting and trustworthy

---

* It's a far cry from the string socks I had vaguely thought I'd make her.

† Also on sale = hurrah!

153

about his face that I blab all about wanting to try out for the show. It's like I'm having an out-of-body experience as I hear myself tell him all about my fears and how I feel I can't NOT try out now, and the song I'm considering and so on.

'I think it's a great idea,' he says, and I can tell he means it. 'You should defo go for it.'

'But it's a secret,' I say. 'You can't tell anyone.' And then, to make this a hundred milliondy times worse, I add, 'Not even Dixie.'

NO! I've said a Bad Thing. *THE* Bad Thing.

We both realize that I have made a secret between our small gang of friends, two against one. I have to take it back but I CAN'T. If Uggs keeps this secret, I have divided us, the Gang, me (and no one else), by asking him to keep this knowledge to himself.

There is a painful silence between us.

I am more miserable than ever. So is Uggs. But if I agree to tell Dixie, then that will make it even MORE real. I'm not sure the Jenny Q nerves can handle that. My bag of quality knitting stuff feels as heavy as concrete as we walk along the street to meet Dixie.

My *BAD*.

154

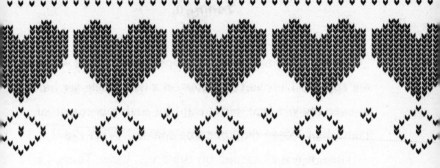

HELL ON WHEELS

My day should have been an adventure and a pleasure. Instead, I am left feeling like a total heel, and rightly so. I have done a bad thing and I am feeling it . . . *acutely.**

I am in a daze as we walk to O'Connell Street and, bless Uggs, he does his best to keep me in touch with the world around us.

'Why are there so many clocks above the shops on this street?' he asks.

Normally that would provoke a fine discussion, a good argument even.

'Would you have chosen a particular shop because you loved their clock?' he wonders.

* Sometimes words sound exactly how they feel and that's one of them = ACUTELY. It sounds like what it means. It hurts.

Dixie is nowhere to be seen and I am glad cos when she appears I'll have to plaster on a lying smile for her all over my vile face. How can I be such a betrayer of friendship? When did I become sneaky? WHY did I?

'They're not all agreed on the time,' I say. 'There's a bit of a difference between them all.'

'Five or ten minutes,' he agrees. 'If you chose the one the buses are ignoring, you'd be out of luck for getting home. There's probably a big philosophical argument waiting to happen right there.'

'Uggs . . .' I start.

'No, Jen, it's OK,' he says. 'You'll tell Dix when you're ready. You don't like being crowded and it's a big thing you're doing. Take your time.'

How can this guy be so great? He's thirteen too, so why can't I be like him?

Dixie slopes out of Primark to the left of us, plastered in make-up – she's obviously let someone[†] loose on her face in a department store earlier. And it's not just make-up; she's clearly also been sprayed by any perfume seller she's passed in the last two hours.

She puts bits of hand and arm up to our noses, saying,

† or several people, actually, now that I'm up close.

'What do you think of that?' The tip of my nose now has a concoction of odours on it and I'm not sure I like any of them.

'Which clock are we going by?' she asks, like she was listening in on some of our previous wonderings. She's in tune with Uggs and me, even if she doesn't know all of what has passed between us. I feel even worse now.

'Not sure we can trust any of them,' Uggs says.

I feel this clock discussion could start mirroring my life and how untrustworthy I am as a friend. If I can't tell all my Bestests what I'm about, how can I be a *true* friend?

THE HEEL OF
HUMANITY

We head to the bus stop and who is waiting for our bus home? Only Stevie Lee & Co. and the EmmyLou Slinky, who is *devoting* herself to the Bolton Boy. He looks like he's loving the attention. I am gutted. Shredded. And I feel I deserve it all.

'She has a sticky-outy chin and a big, pointy nose,' Dix says and, instead of laughing at her fabtasticness, I want to burst into loud, repentant sobs, telling her what a low-life I am and a bad, BAD friend.

What's great, though, is that she's right: there is a certain amount of pointy-ness to the EmmySlinky face.* I love Dixie for saying it, which, in turn, makes me feel awful all over again.

* Thank you, Nature!

I am not worthy!

'She's SO not All That,' Dix continues, oblivious to my discomfort at how life is showing me up to be (frankly) a SHIZZ.

'NOT all that, *fact*,' Uggs says.

I am a HEEL, a paring from the rough, scaly, dry skin of the sole of Humanity. They are the shiny, bright nail-varnish-newly-applied-to pedicured feet that are really so lovely they don't even need a pedicure at all.

The bus comes. (On time, according to one city-centre clock, surely?) We go upstairs, as do all the Oakdale peeps, but this time I don't play with the window or any passing branches of trees – I have done my bit for the amusement of humankind today. Mostly, I want to be home, safe, hidden.

It's a rattly journey and the sound of laughter from the back seat[†] is enough to make me want to throw myself off this vehicle at a high speed. Dixie is discussing underwear with Uggs and I'm pretending to be involved too, though I have a horrid buzzing in my head and I feel really shaky. She's fallen in love with some peacock colours that she assures us are IT this season. She

---

† Her/Slinky = tinkly, him/Hunk = throaty.

159

doesn't seem to have got any inspiration for handmade gifts unless she's going to make bras and knickers for her family and, really, knowing Dixie, I would not put that past her.

'Dark rich jade, deep royal blue,' she gushes.

They do sound lovely. I'll bet EmmyLou Slinky has such a combination of undies on, because the Slinkies are SO up to the minute fashion-wise.

The Cool People get off the stop before us, no doubt headed away to be utterly fabulous. The Less Cool of us get off closer to home.

'I think I'd best do a trial of the bath bombs,' Uggs says. 'How about we go for that tomorrow?'

It's a great idea.

'Can it not be my house?' I say. 'ONLY cos who knows what crazy pregnancy craving Mum will have by then. She might want to eat the bombs and, though they're made of good stuff, the fizziness might not suit the baby.'

There are nods all round at this wisdom. We all remember the time the class put Mentos into a big bottle of diet cola and it made a gigantic, explosive spurt of effervescence into the air and covered everything in sugary, sticky stuff. Then someone (Mike Hussy, to name names) had to go one better and did it using his own body as the experimental container and the result was THE most spectacular vomit I have ever seen, or ever will see, I suspect.[‡] It was PROJECTILE. I'm glad I was not the person standing in front of him – that was Hugo Pheifer and I'm not sure he has recovered yet.

Gypsy is waiting at the bus stop. You'd think Uggs had phoned ahead to tell her when we'd be arriving. She starts leaping and barking and being generally delighted to see us back, safe and well.

'Do you think a nice, cherry-red will suit Gyp?' he asks.

It's only then I see he has a bag from the great wool shop. I was so wrapped up and selfish that I didn't notice him buy something there too.

Then he starts singing to her, to the tune, and vaguely the words, of that song 'Zip-A-Dee-Doo-Dah' that we all heard as kids.

---

‡ Although I hear that babies are good at this kind of thing.

'Gyp-a-dee-doo-dah, Gyp-a-dee-ay,
What a great dog you are s'all I can say!
Plenty of treatses comin' your way,
Gyp-a-dee-doo-dah, Gyp-a-dee-ay!'

For the first time in my life, I want to be that dog.

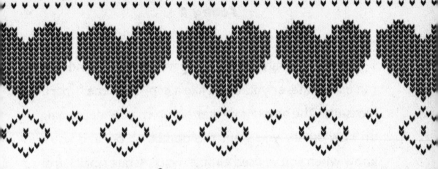

EUGENE'S BATH BOMBS

INGREDIENTS

Citric acid
Bicarbonate of soda
Cornflour
Essential oils
Water to bind all of the above

SCIENCE BIT

The science bit of Uggs's bath bombs is as follows: citric acid reacts with the bicarbonate of soda in the presence of water (i.e. your bath) to produce carbon dioxide, which gives the bath bombs their fizz = RESULT! You are experiencing DA BOMB.

The ratio of ingredients should be 2 parts citric acid,

1 part bicarbonate of soda, 1 part cornflour, and you can use whatever you want, like a cup, to be the '1 part' measure. The amount of scent is up to you, depending on how smelly you want the bombs to be, and you'll know when you've used enough water (start small here) when you have a good consistency going (you don't want it too wet!).

METHOD

Sieve the bicarbonate of soda into a bowl, then add the citric acid and cornflour and mix well. Add the scent and some water and mix those well also. Then put into the moulds you've chosen and leave to set. We used a muffin tray to shape the bombs but you could use anything you fancy. Put the mixture in bit by bit and press down to keep the bomb nice and solid.

The finished bombs could be wrapped in grease-proof paper then tied at the top with string or ribbon. Just be sure to keep them dry till they go into your bath.*

* Do not allow the saliva of Gyp-like creatures to make contact.

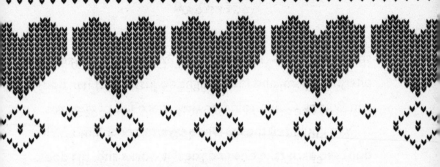

FAIR TRADE

'These are easily as good as anything you can buy in a shop,' Dixie says.

She's right.

We are sitting in Uggs's house and are well pleased with ourselves.

'Perhaps we should try adding colour next time?' Uggs says, going all professional and perfectionist.

'What if that stains the bath?' I suggest, remembering some stuff Dad brought home to test out on us, the Quinns, his very own 'lab rats'. In particular an orange one left us, as well as the bath, looking like we'd been Tangoed.

'I quite like the natural look of them,' Dixie says. 'They smell and look *healthy*.'

I'm glad we didn't make them at mine because they

smell good and citrusy enough to make you want to bite into them, and Mum might do just that if her body and Bumpy Quinn told her they were full of vitamins.

'We could sell these,' Dixie says, 'no problemo. Why don't we each take one and see if it works and, if it does, we'll draw up a business plan?'

A BUSINESS PLAN????

She sees our shocked faces. 'We've gotta move with the times, guys. Trust me. I'm having one of my visionary days.'

Dixie's visions might lead to troubles and it's hard to know how this one could pan out.

We take our bombs and arrange to text results later.

'I want synchronized bathing,' Dix says, like it's an Olympic sport. 'Plus top reportage with marks out of ten.'

She's on a mission . . .

In my bath later, the fizz is fabulous, so that's the first thing I share: **Fizz Factor = 10/10!**

Dix texts: **Smelltastic!**

I go: **MARKS?!**

Dix: **full 10.**

Uggs: **amazeballs, tanx!**

Fair Trade

A strange number texts: **good job well dun Uggs.**

Me: **who dis?**

Unknown: **Gypsy**

Well, Uggs has finally lost it. He has got the hound her own mobile. I just really hope it's not her doing the texting because that would be so shocking as to make me retire from life. Strangely, I can imagine her pointy little nails hitting the numbers and letters on a phone – most disturbing.

I send back: **o course! stupid o me nt 2 guess.**

Then I kind of kick myself, mentally, because I have just texted a dog, even if I meant my message to be dripping in gentle scorn. It's not just Uggs who's losing it.

Gypsy texts: **DUH!**

I have to smack my forehead to knock some sense into my head. When we get over the madness of a texter being a dog, supposedly, we score v v high marks for the bombs.*

When I go downstairs Mum says, 'That's given the whole house a lovely, zingy smell.'

I text: **zing factor 10/10.**

* v good fragrance, fizz and lingering afterwhiff.

Gran says, 'Froooteeeee', Dad gives, 'Bang on,' and even Dermo goes, 'Yeah, not bad.'[†]

Dix: **Da Bomb is born! Now need celeb endorsement.**

We all text **SLINKIES** to one another at the same time, so hopefully that means 'great minds think alike' and Gyp goes: **woof!** Seems we're going into business. Uggs has scored a totally tub-tastic hit.

Of course, human nature means I now feel v v inadequate by comparison, so I get to work on my knitted projects. There is no time to lose and every stitch counts. Plus the problem with knitting is that it does soak up time and the results are not as immediate as with a bath bomb. There is also the fact that I am a low, crawling thing, unworthy of friendship, and that has not gone away.

'You smell good enough to bite,' Mum tells me, and I know for sure I made the right decision taking the bath-bomb production out of our house. The temptation would have been too much for her. She would *so* have tried to scoff one.

† V high praise from him.

CRIMESTOPPERS

The kitchen clears and I ask, 'Mum, is keeping something from your friends the same as lying?'

'Well, people keep things to themselves for all sorts of reasons. Maybe they think they'll make a situation worse if they share, or maybe they feel it's not their place to interfere. And that wouldn't mean LYING, though there is such a thing as "a sin of omission" and it'd be like an *error* of omission in ordinary life. All depends on the circumstances, I suppose.'

I nod and I bet I look miserable.

'Does a friend of yours have a problem of this sort?' she asks.

'Yes. A friend is keeping something from one of his best friends because he's afraid of being laughed at, but it'll cause a big hoohah if it comes out. And he's also told his other best friend, so they're both in a bad place now.'

Surely the fact I said the pal is a HE will throw her off the scent – I am pleased with this even if, technically, it's likely to be a lie too.

'This friend should probably balance up the good with the bad. Maybe to be laughed at a little bit might not be such a bad thing and it would be meant affectionately, I'd say, if they're true friends. It might be gentler than risking, say, losing a best friend. Making decisions like this is all part of growing up, Jen, of taking responsibility.'

I am more miserable now than ever before.

'For your friend, that is. Obviously it's not you.'

'No. Not me.'

Gran saunters in. 'Cheer up, Jen, it might never happen,' she says.

I'm saved from saying anything because the Quinns are gathering for one of our favourite shows and there is plenty else to think about. We stock up on chocolate and crisps and gather on the sofas and armchairs.

One of the strange things about going back to school is that it coincides with the television getting good again. So, just when you have less time to watch it because you have homework and all, the programmes get better

= Sod's Law. The Quinns have several, separate favourites but some shows are meant to be watched and enjoyed all together, and one of those is *Crimestoppers*. That's exactly what we're tucking into now, as well as cheese 'n' onion crisps and Maltesers.*

Crimestoppers is an hour long and you can ring in to the studio with information on the crimes if you have any. Real police present it and they are v wooden, telling us about the awful stuff that's happened in Ireland during the week. As well as criminals doing stupidly awful stuff too. I'd say presenting the show is way harder for the cops than going out chasing the villains.

The best thing is when we absorb the facts and then Dad turns and says, 'And where were YOU on the night of Wednesday 7 August?'

Then you have to have a really good alibi or he might have to phone up the programme and turn you in. I nearly got caught for an armed robbery in Co. Tipperary once because I had such a lame excuse involving Dixie and a knitting lesson.

Gran often confesses but Dad just can't bring himself

* on top of the bath bomb, my hands now smell very strange.

171

to hand her over, or that's what he says. And sometimes, if it looks like he will, Mum will make a big plea on behalf of Gran and beg him not to turn her in. I keep waiting for a dog story so that I can anonymously shop Gypsy for a crime she may, or may not, have committed.

Sometimes we like to guess who in the Oakdale area might be suited to a certain crime, but then you have to pick the person least likely EVER to do such a thing and back up your theory TO THE HILT. The strangest people might be criminal masterminds, according to the Quinns.

Gran is particularly devious and good at this activity. One night, we saw a piece about a stolen articulated lorry full of live chickens.

'Rosie O'Rourke from Beech Close,' Gran said. 'Can't help herself. It's in her blood. Countrywoman. Can't resist livestock. Been rustling poultry since she was three feet high.'

'She's in a mobility scooter now,' Mum pointed out.

'Deep cover,' Gran assured her. 'She only uses that thing for show in her leisure hours; rest of the time she's like Lara Croft, throwing herself around, beating up on people and stealing chickens left right and centre. Besides, where *was* she on the night of 3 September?'

crimestoppers

I'm nearly sure Mrs O'Rourke is ninety-seven.

Tonight, there's the usual mix of attacks, car theft, cashpoint robberies and an item on con artists scamming people out of their savings by being charming and not who they seem to be. I keep expecting my face to flash up on the screen as the biggest hoaxer[†] in Oakdale.

There's an item on a bunny rabbit belonging to a homeless man being chucked into the River Liffey in town – what a terrible thing to do. The man jumped in and saved his pet and then they were both rescued from the river by the fire brigade.

Dad turns to Dermot and asks, 'Where were YOU on that Saturday?'

I'm glad it wasn't me he picked on because I WAS in town that day! Dermot has a brilliant alibi because it turns out he was part of an unreported heist on a yoghurt factory in Monaghan that day.

Although it's a great episode, and the Quinns do well with their excuses, I go to sleep troubled. I dream that Dixie is a giant bath bomb and I throw her into a giant bath and she fizzes away to nothing, shouting, 'I'm your

† OK. I'll admit I am DEEPLY paranoid at the moment.

173

friend. I smell of grapefruit. How could you do this to me?' Gypsy is barking, barking, barking. Then I wake. I am all sweaty and sticky and my heart is RACING, and I smell of grapefruit too. And Gypsy is barking, so maybe I didn't dream that bit. Actually, I'm vaguely grateful to Gypsy for waking me, as I really didn't want to continue dreaming that dream and who knows how much longer it would have taken to run out. I might have pulled the plug on Dixie and flushed her away.

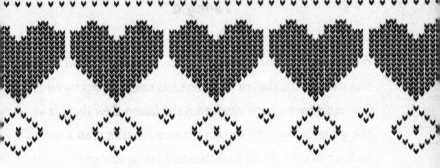

THE MORNING AFTER
THE NIGHT BEFORE

I slouch into breakfast.

Gran says, 'You look like you were dragged back-wards through a bush, missy.'

It's not a massively helpful comment, so I just grunt at her, which I know is acceptable as I'm a teen. Then I hide behind my fringe, which I am growing a) to be cool and b) to use to hide behind – double whammy result.

I also hate being called 'missy' and I'm sure Gran knows that and does it deliberately to rile me. She's *good* at that kind of torture.

Mum is drinking something green with chunks in it and to be honest it looks like peppermint puke, though I strongly suspect it may have gherkin in it and is probably not minty at all. I don't ask what it's made of as that's a need-to-know basis and I SO don't need to know, not this early in the day, or ever. She has taken to sitting with her hand contentedly resting on the Bump. Every so often she goes, 'Whoo, this one's a mover,' as she feels a little kick or punch. It's all a bit much, a bit upsetting.

I still feel odd that there is a small person growing in my mum's tum, but I admit it's getting less freaky now and there is a general excitement in the house that we'll have a baby before long, just a few months. OK, I'll admit it: I'm warming to the idea, in spite of the jumping in the tum bit and the ghastly gherkins.

Dermot is acting shifty, like he's hiding something. I know, I know, I'm one to talk, BUT I recognize *concealment* in others now, like I have gained an unwanted superpower. He's avoiding questions, dodging conversation and looks like he's UP TO SOMETHING. Everyone else thinks it's because he's sixteen and that's what blokes do when they're that age.

This morning he's acting *fascinated* by his Rice Krispies as they snap, crackle and pop. It's as if he wants us to think he can understand some mysterious thing they're sharing with him. Yeah, right – as I say, he's UP TO SOMETHING.

The Morning After the Night Before

Today, he's taking his guitar to school, saying it's for Guitar Club, though no one asked him, so that's Too Much Information right there and a sure sign that he wants us to believe something that is not fully the truth.* Looks like we've all got secrets of some sort.

I'm happy enough with that. Some secrets should remain, well, secret. Like, I have no interest in knowing Gran's,† or Dad's or Mum's. In a way I'm still a bit queasy that so many people know a big thing about us Quinns, because they can see the Bump growing daily before their eyes.

But the Dermot one is of interest to me, intriguing me, you might say, because it may involve Stevie Lee Bolton, so it is my business, as a result, when you think about it. It also makes me feel a teeny tiny weeny bit better about myself and that helps a teeny tiny weeny bit.

* I happen to know when Guitar Club is because SLB takes it too and if that makes me a stalker, so be it.
† Gran did tell me a secret once, but it primarily involved her dentures, and so I have not ventured into 'secrets' territory with her again.

177

MR BOMBTASTIC

Already Dixie is all over the business plan like a rash, which is exactly what we're all glad we did not wake up with this morning.* Dixie has morphed into a dynamo, even her uniform looks like a power suit now, so maybe this new bath product has powers we don't yet know of.

'What we do is give her a bomb and say we'd love her feedback and then, when she loves it, we encourage her to tell all her friends and we tell anyone who'll listen. Perfect word-of-mouth marketing and FREE.'

'Which one?' I ask.

'Which one what?'

'Which Slinky?'

'Samantha. I think she's the natural leader there.'

---

* our product has passed yet another test.

Uggs is looking sheepish.

'Wots the happs?'† Dixie wants to know.

Uggs does an Ugg Shrug. 'I'm not sure I'm ready to be a businessman. I'm more the shy inventor type.'

Dixie raises an eyebrow. 'There are three kinds of people in this world, Uggs – those who make things happen, those who let things happen, and those who wonder what the hell just happened.'

I'm not sure what her point is but it does sound mega-impressive.

'Have you got it?' Dixie asks.

'Well, I get the –'

'The bath bomb, Uggs, not the concept.'

'Oh, yes.'

He produces a wrapped one. 'I've gone with the whole kitchen theme. I put the bomb itself into a paper muffin case then used unbleached baking paper as a wrap and string to tie it off.'

It looks superb, pretty but with a healthy, natural vibe. I'm a little bit in love with it and it smells great, even if that reminds me of my dream.

† Where did THAT come from? She's not usually into that kind of lingo and v quick to mock those who are.

179

We wait in the schoolyard till Sam Slinky is more or less alone, or at least not in conversation with anyone, and we go over to her.[‡] Dixie is bolder than Uggs and me but she says I must open the conversation on account of Sam going out with my brother. EEK!

My voice sounds ridiculous, like I have swallowed helium, as I go, 'Morning, Sam.'

She looks startled, so I'd say the Gang must look a bit weird – eyes poppy-outy with not knowing how this will go and gawky with having dared engage an older goddess type.

Dixie takes over. 'We were wondering, I mean we'd absolutely love it, if you'd try out a sample of our bath bombs for us and tell us what you think.'

Uggs holds forth the offering in both hands with an imploring expression, like Oliver Twist holding up his bowl for more. I nearly giggle at how mad it must all look.

'We've tried them,' I say. 'And they're super. Well, we think they are. Like fruity and fizzy and fresh.'

'Erm, sure,' Samantha says, with a *really* puzzled look now.

She takes the bomb like it might be an actual explo-

‡ or rather approach Her Royal Slinkiness.

sive and nervously sniffs it, then smiles. 'Grapefruit, excellent.'

'Thanks,' Dixie says and herds us away, probably worried that I'll make another speech, or Uggs will find his voice. In fact, as we turn the corner she hisses, 'Run, before she changes her mind.'

Phase One of Operation Celebrity Endorsement is go.

I see Stevie Lee going into the school with Peter Gowen and they're both carrying guitars. Maybe Guitar Club has moved days after all. I'll have to check. How bad is it that I automatically thought Dermot was up to something, because I'm so suspicious and willing to see the worst in everyone, all because I am involved in lying?

I have a prime example of lowness to compare myself to as we get to our classroom. Mike Hussy is blocking the door and giving grief to all who want to get in. He's poking Teddy Thompson very hard in the soft bit just under his shoulder and that's gotta hurt.

Teddy is a small, floppy-haired geek who wears glasses to round off the look. He's really cute, actually, and smart and nice, and quiet, and Uggs really likes him. He looks nine years old. Mike looks like a giant troll beside him.

I see red. Perhaps because I am feeling guilty myself, I march up to Hussy and say, 'Pick on someone your own size,' which (as usual) is not very original but at least he stops poking Teddy.

Hussy turns to me and barges at me with his chest out, again and again. 'Think you're big enough, so, do you?' he shouts on each barge. He bumps me once more and I fall over, yelping at the sharp pain as my bottom hits the ground hard.

I feel tears sting my eyes. 'You gonna start beating up girls now too?' I shout. 'What a *big* man you are.' I stagger to my feet, my bag threatening to pull me down again. I hear him mutter to his cronies, 'It must be that time of the month.'

'What did you just say?' I ask him.

'It's private, between me and my friends,' he says.

'They're not your friends!' I shout. 'They hang around with you because they're afraid of you.'

Hussy looks suspiciously at his posse now but they do the 'she's mad' look. He turns back and deliberately unbalances me as I try to get past him.

'Bog off, Mike,' Dixie says. 'You can't bully all of us, all at once.'

This is a tremendous point and one we should remember always. There are more of us than him and, if we band together, surely he can't continue his utterly bad behaviour.

I seethe through the morning, though, and get caught by the teachers a few times 'daydreaming' and am ticked off, which fuels my anger. I catch Hussy sniggering at that. I might knit a doll of him and pinch it a lot, in case that might be of benefit for someone, anyone.

At break, Uggs says, 'What would happen if we were all really *nice* to Mike? You know, laugh when he says something awful as if he's really amusing, tell him it's great to see him every day, and ignore him and walk away if he gets mean.'

'High risk,' Delia Thomas says. 'It might really annoy him.'

'Could be worth the risk, just to see,' Maya says.

Everyone nods. It'll kill me to be civil to Hussy, let alone nice, but, if that's the general agreement, I'll try it.

I see on the school notice board that Guitar Club

hasn't moved and that lowers my mood even further. What's Dermot up to and what part does SLB play in his nefarious[6] plan?

6 I know, could that sound any better? It means criminal, more or less. Actually, they should use it on crimestoppers because they overuse heinous and grievous, and nefarious would make a nice change.

KNIT WITS

'Names, names, names,' Dixie demands that afternoon.

'Grape Expectations?' I suggest, pleased that I have invoked literature there with a nod to Dickens.

'Nice,' says Dixie, scribbling it down. 'What other varieties might we offer our customers?'

'A Hippy Dippy, using patchouli?' Uggs suggests. 'And the Great Calm, using lavender?'

'Good, good,' Dixie says, writing those down too.

'And a Flower Power using rose oil?' I suggest. 'Mums and Grans seem to like that.'

'I think we should keep our menu short and concentrate on quality,' Dixie says, and that makes sense.

'Overall the product could be called Da Bomb?' I suggest.

We all agree on that.

We're knitting and knattering in my room, though only myself and Uggs are working on tangible projects. I'm click-clacking away like a mad thing on Dad's skinny tie because it needs to be v v long. Uggs is working his lovely deep-red wool and looking worried. Dixie and Gypsy are just up for mischief.

'Do you think it'll spoil the surprise if I let Gyp see what I'm knitting?' Uggs asks.

'No,' I say. I'd love to add something acid and pithy on the end of this but that might be as sad as the fact that he has asked that question.

'She's a dog,' Dixie says, with a frown.

'Exactly,' Uggs says, as if he has proved a point.

I'm not getting involved in this discussion.

'Dix, I hate to bring this up but you don't seem to have a plan for presents.'

She sighs. 'I know. I'm not motivated on that yet.'

'Are we going to have a major panic and crisis week before Christmas?' I ask, leadingly.

'Nah, it'll come: the inspiration. Always does, you know.'

'Yes, but what about sheer time scale?' I say, with mild doom in my voice.

Knit Wits

'I can always buy Bombs,' she says.

'Lazy, Dixiegal.'

'But brilliant, Jenpal. It's what I'm hoping everyone else in the school does. Then we'll be in the money and all will be eurotastic in our world.'

'Or yoyotastic,' Uggs says, because he likes to call euros yoyos, and Gypsy barks at the sound of his voice.*

'You know the rule, you can't sit in this craft circle without something on needles,' I say.

'OK, OK.' She rummages in her (huge) bag – all but disappears into it – then emerges with a hairy yarn† that has a variety of turquoises in it. It's lovely. It will knit up into waves of colour and be, well, hairy.

'Cushion cover for Mum,' she tells us, 'with big buttons in a contrasting colour on the back.'

'Genius,' I say.

'Yup, told you the inspiration would strike.'

She did, it has.

---

* or maybe she agrees with him. Hard to tell.

† Dix says that, technically, it's called an eyelash yarn. Gross.

'What do we know about Mike Hussy?' I ask, still bugged by the (_I_).

'He's a pain,' Dixie says.

'A jerk,' Uggs adds.

'A bully,' I say. 'But why?'

'How do you mean, why?' Uggs asks. 'Why what?'

'Why is he a bully?'

'Some people just are,' Dixie says, with a shrug.

'Mum thinks he may have issues we don't know about.'

'Whatever they are I wish he'd sort them out,' Uggs says.

'No excuse for being so mean,' Dixie says.

'That's what I think too,' I say.

'Great minds think alike,' Dixie tells me, with a smile.

'So, we kick Operation Charm Mike into proper action tomorrow?' Uggs says.

'Yup,' Dixie says.

'I have a bad feeling about it,' I say.

'I don't think we have any alternative, unless we go to war with him, with actual fighting,' Uggs says. 'I'm so not into that.'

Dixie confirms. 'We're lovers not fighters.'

Knit Wits

We mull over the Mike Situation for a while in near silence, with just the hushed clack of needles making stitches.

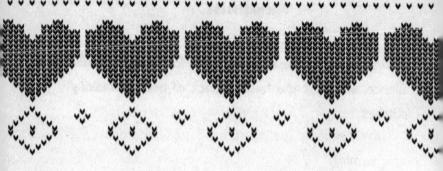

THE ADMISSION

Dixie decides to get philosophical. 'If only life could be like knitting,' she says, sort of sighing and looking tortured by the braininess of her observation.

Uggs and I murmur and nod a bit, not knowing where she'll go with this. There's a silence, then I give in and ask, 'How do you mean?'

'Well, just look at the label on your wool. Everything you need to know is there, like what size needles to use, what colour batch the ball belongs to. All the clues are there to help you, if you want them. It's a shame there's no such manual for life.'

'Mmm,' is all I can manage, because I think I might burst out laughing at how serious she's got. I can't look her in the eye. Uggs is having a bit of a coughing fit.*

* Also laughter-related if you ask me.

The Admission

'I can't believe you're not going for *Teen Factor X*,' Dixie says, sharply changing the focus of the conversation.

'ME?' I squeak. I've got to hand it to her, I didn't see that coming.

'Yeah, you,' Dixie says, laughing. 'Who did you think I meant? Uggs and Gypsy doing some sort of routine?'

Uggs goes all red and Dixie pounces: 'I don't believe it, Uggs. You really did consider that, didn't you?'

'She's really smart and talented,' he stammers. 'But we decided we didn't want to be in the public eye.'

Dixie hoots with laughter and falls on to her back, kicking her feet in the air with merriment. I give Uggs a look that I hope says, 'See? That's what I'm trying to avoid.'

When she recovers, she grills me again.

'I don't fancy it,' I say, busying myself with picking up a stitch I dropped in fright.

There is another silence.

'Oh,' she finally says, and it's a hurt sound. 'You so *are* going for it. And you weren't going to tell me.'

There is an awkward silence.

'Don't be stupid,' I say, without meeting her eyes.

191

'You are,' she repeats. 'You're going to audition for it.'

I look up and see the expression on Dixie's face and it cuts through me and I want to curl up and hide for ever and a day.

'I can't believe it,' she says. 'We tell each other everything.'

Another painful silence.

She looks at Uggs. He goes even redder. 'You knew,' she says, in a dull voice.

'It's all my fault,' I say. 'I was afraid you'd make fun of me but I HAD to tell someone, so Uggs was it. And even that was accidental. No one else knows.'

She nods but I know things are now not OK, at ALL. I am a coward and a liar and I may be about to lose my Best Gal Pal. She will *so* defriend me for this.

'I'm sorry, Dix,' I say, and I have never meant anything so much in my whole life.

I look at Uggs and he can't meet my eyes. Neither can Gyp. He told the dog!

He sees my mind at work and he mutters, 'She can keep a secret.'

I very much doubt it. I don't trust that mutt. And

The Admission

now Dixie doesn't trust me any more because I didn't trust her. I stare down at my knitting needles in shame. I am well and truly stitched up with this, and it's nobody's fault but my own.

CHARM SCHOOL

I walk to school alone the following day. My choice. Uggs calls at my house for me but I lie, again.* I say I'm not ready and he should go on ahead without me, so he does. There is no contact from Dixie and, though that wouldn't normally be a worry, I can't help reading utter doom into it today. When she left last night she was subdued. We all were. I hope she can forgive me. I don't know what to do to make it up to her.

I've decided that I just can't schmooze Mike Hussy with charm, or anything else, so my plan is to stay out of his orbit and not get involved. I'll smile and walk away if I'm caught near him. What I really want to do is to

---

* I seem to be getting good at it, or natural-sounding, anyhow, and that's BAD, i.e. the rocky road to ruin.

punch him in his mush, and that's unacceptable, and I know it would feel fine for a moment but it would be stooping to his level. Besides, who am I to think I can judge others when I am clearly so SO flawed myself?

I see Dix a good length ahead of me on the street before school and I call to her and she turns around and waves (good) but she doesn't stop to wait for me (bad). Delia and Maya come round a corner and she hooks up with them. I am gutted but I deserve it, so boo-hoo, Jenny Q. I've been glad until now that Delia and Maya get on so well because I don't feel so guilty about not letting them properly join our gang of three.[†] But now I see them with Dixie and I feel agitated by it, in a negative way.

Uggs is lying in wait for me. He's so loyal and I don't deserve that either. He smiles and I know he's trying to cheer me up but truth is I'm a moody Q today. I also happen to know that my hair has gone big and fuzzy and I didn't have time, or the inclination, to try to tame it. I look like a clown and I am most certainly a fool.

'Turn that frown upside down,' Uggs says. 'Remember, we have a charm offensive to set in motion.'

---

† Gypsy still SO does not count in my eyes.

195

Before I can explain my plan to avoid Mike Hussy, Sam Slinky appears and comes over.

'Guys, I just LOVED the bath bomb. Well done. Great idea and you should SO, like, sell them.'

That makes me beam. I can't wait to tell Dixie.

Uggs looks shocked but recovers himself well. 'Thanks so much for road testing it, Sam. Tell your friends. We'll certainly take orders if anyone would like some at a great price.' He's in smooth business mode. 'We have other varieties if you'd like to try some more?'

'Absolutely. I'll be, like, your guinea pig, yeah?'

Sam Slinky could not look less like a guinea pig if she tried, but it's a truly amusing idea.[‡] Apparently, if you are nervous or v shy of someone, you should imagine them sitting on the loo, but that just makes me laugh nervously and then feel even more discombobulated.

'We're in business,' Uggs says as Sam walks[6] away. Then, 'Flippin flapjacks, what have we just got ourselves into?'

'The money, hopefully.'

[‡] I try to picture her with a furry little face but it's not working.

[6] or slinks.

charm school

We rush to tell our Business Manager and she's pleased, even if she manages to avoid meeting my eyes.

'We'd best make some stock,' she says. 'Planning meeting hereby called for this afternoon after school.'

'At mine?' I ask.

'Natch,' she says. 'That's where the Kit Kats live.'

That lifts me a little. It will do. It's something to build on. And right now I couldn't care less about *Teen Factor X*, I just want to make things right with my friend again. This grief is not worth it.

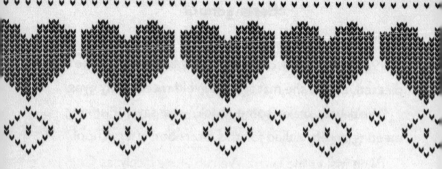

THE BIG BANG

I watch the others try to schmooze Mike Hussy for the day but he's like a brick wall. He snarls at every smile. He does look confused that people are being polite and nice to him, even though he doesn't return that 'compliment' and he deliberately pushes others around as if it's an accident as often as possible.

It's worst at Phys Ed when we're playing volleyball in the schoolyard. Then we're all targets. He deliberately aims the ball at bodies, for or against his team, and thumps into anyone close by at any opportunity. He's hateful. I am not a violent person AT ALL but he makes me want to lash out. I try to use that in my game, to channel it, but I'm not very good at volleyball anyhow and this doesn't help.

I can't concentrate properly on classes because of

the situation with Dixie. Life things take over my brain,* like why are me and Dixie friends? Yup, it's BIG stuff. I've never really thought about that before. I suppose I never had to.

Dixie makes me laugh. We rub along nicely, as Gran would say. She's sort of like the sister I don't have.† I can't find any one thing that explains it. Sometimes you realize that love is unanalysable – soppy as it is, I do *love* Dixie. And I love Uggs too, for all the same reasons. Sometimes he's creepily good and nice, though, and it would be satisfying to pinch him. Dixie is a bit more wicked than that. They're a good blend of friends.

We're just outside the school ready to go home when Teddy goes by on his bike. He smiles at us. He passes Mike Hussy & Co. and says, 'See you tomorrow, Mike,' and Hussy just pushes him over, off his bike, on to the road.

Everything seems to slow down with the shock of what we are witnessing.

---

* I miss most of the French Revolution in History class as a result, and there was I thinking we didn't do enough about other countries.

† Yet: the Bump could be a girl, Mum's not saying.

199

Teddy leans to the side further and further. He takes his hands off the handlebars to break his fall. The bike hits the ground with a crash of metal. Poor Teddy is tangled up in the frame. A car screams to a halt right in front of him, only inches from his head. He could have been killed!

It's like I snap back into real time and that's it. I've had enough of Hussy: he's gone way too far this time. Dixie and Uggs help Teddy up and I run back into the school to the principal's office. I am going to report Hussy and I don't give a fig what the consequences are. I am panting, gasping for breath and starting to cry by the time I knock on Mr Bradley's door.

I babble what's happened and he tells me to calm down before he rushes out of the office. A group has gathered around the incident and everyone is willing to name Mike Hussy as the villain who did this. He'll be suspended or expelled and I don't care because he deserves punishment (though not having to go to school would probably suit him just fine). He's nowhere to be seen, of course, the big coward.

Teddy is fine, his legs and hands are a bit grazed, but he was going slowly when he was knocked over and he had a helmet on. He's more shaken than anything else. The poor motorist is in a state too. Teddy's mum[‡] is on the way to collect him now and he's adamant that he doesn't need an ambulance – we can all see that he's mortified to be the centre of such fuss and attention. Mr Bradley takes details and then goes to deal with Hussy.

'Mike Hussy is in deep, smelly doodah now,' Uggs says.

'At least we can give up being nice to him,' I say.

'Yeah, it was getting on my chest to be so pleasant to him,' Dixie admits.

‡ When she arrives, Teddy's mum is like a tiny owl, and very angry that someone tried to harm her chick. I wouldn't like to cross her when she's like this. And I really wouldn't want to be Mike Hussy when she gets her hands/claws on him.

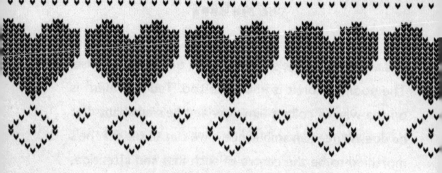

OUT OUT OUT

Mike Hussy has been suspended and our class, and the whole school, is a happier place without him. I think other years that may have bullies are reaping some benefit because everyone is on their best behaviour for a while. His clique of pals is subdued and that's a good thing too. They look ashamed and so they should be: they are accessories to a crime. However, as Mum has advised me, it does not do to gloat, so there's no smugness allowed for those of us who are glad that the right thing seems to have been done.

If only I could be totally right again with Dixie.

Mr Bradley gives us a speech at Assembly about how the school has a 'zero-tolerance policy' with regard to bullying or any other sort of threatening behaviour. He looks like he loves this crisis. He does make one cracking point that teachers can't help if they don't know what's going on, but that doesn't cover the fact that you'd look like a snitch if you went running tattling tales. Thankfully no one thinks I'm a snitch for going to him about Mike Hussy, because he had nearly been the cause of very serious bodily harm.

Teddy says Mike was made to apologize to him personally but that it was all a bit weird because Mike and his mum looked really scared as they were walking away, even though Mike should be delighted to be off school for a while and that the police aren't involved. Teddy puffed his chest out a little as he said, 'I'm not pressing charges,' and he looked megacute.

Teen Factor X auditions are this weekend and it is a banned subject for discussion. None of the Gang said that 'rule' out loud, it's just clear that this is the best way to progress. Of course, now that both Uggs and Dixie know, the sensible thing would be for them to come with me, but that can't happen. I have been a fool and we'd all lose face if I asked them because then they'd be forced to accompany me and maybe they wouldn't want to be seen with a total EEJIT.

Thankfully we have a lot of other work to tackle,

namely DA BOMB. Uggs wants to try out the other recipes we're proposing and we agree that Sam Slinky should be given samples of those as our Celebrity Endorser. Also, if we have stock, we can fill any orders we might get quicker.

It's a lot of fun in the kitchen as Uggs calls for ingredients and we go, 'Yes chef!' We're getting along fine but there is an invisible barrier that we all feel and it's my fault. If I tear at that by trying to be all big and tackling the problem I've made head-on, I worry that I will ruin what we have altogether. I am going to see how we get on and, *IF* the time is ever right to talk to Dix about how dreadful I have been, I will.

The weekend is looming and I'm not sleeping well. I wake at 5 a.m. most mornings, even before Gypsy starts her barking routine next door. I lie there listening to the sounds of birds (v noisy) and people going to work early or maybe coming home from a night shift, roaring past on motorbikes or starting cars, and Mum going in and out of the loo a lot.* I'm usually too tired to knit or read or do anything much but lie there and worry.

* Bumpy Quinn is getting big and pressing on all sorts of inside bits now, including Mum's bladder - eeeuw!

204

out out out

And hum. I'm trying out songs in secret and using choir practice as stealth rehearsal for performing in public. At breakfast each morning Gran tells me my eyes are like two holes burnt in a blanket.[†]

† she has a way with words.

QUEUE FOR Q

When Saturday comes I slip out of the house and everyone thinks I'm off to meet Dixie and Uggs. I skulk along the road to the bus stop and then have to duck back and lurk because all of Oakdale seems to be getting the bus to town. Dermot is there with some of his mates and he's got his guitar and then it hits me – he's trying out for the show. It never occurred to me that another Quinn would be interested in that. I have been ultra wrapped up in myself. But right now I don't feel any sympathy for him, more annoyance that I didn't spot this plan earlier so that I could prepare for my brother being in the audition queue too.

I decide to get the later bus, which means I have twenty minutes to kill – the longest twenty of my life. It's hard to waste time when you have nothing to do.

I walk around the streets trying to look like I'm going somewhere and getting more and more wound up. This audition is a really BAD plan, I decide, but I have to go through with it now because Uggs and Dixie know: oh, the irony of that! I pass a house with toys in a top window – there's Woody and Buzz from *Toy Story* and some dolls and bears, and I wish I was still at the age when I could play with those. I'd be happier, that's for sure.

I start to worry that I've picked the wrong clothes to wear. I couldn't choose anything that looked too dressed up because the household would have pounced on that and asked why and also I don't want to look like I made too much effort, so I'm in a white T-shirt, a long floaty skirt and a cropped denim jacket. It's nice, without screaming, I'M HERE TO GET FAMOUS – PICK ME! (I hope). I also have a teensy bit of make-up on – concealer on my spotty chin and a swipe of mascara, as well as some lip gloss.

I somehow manage to flitter away the twenty minutes and sneak back to the bus stop. I wait for all the other passengers to get on the bus and then I sneak on last and sit at the back downstairs. I have brought a book to hide behind but trying to read in a moving vehicle just makes me want to throw up, which does nothing for my shredded nerves. I think I'm safe from meeting anyone I know when I get off in town, but who's ahead of me on the street but Maya and Delia Thomas. I play all cool.

'Yeah, I'm just getting some more wool for the things I'm knitting for Christmas presents,' I say.

'We're going to the *Teen Factor X* auditions,' Maya says.

Without thinking, I squawk, 'WHY?'

'Delia's got a stand-up routine she's going to do.'

'WHAT?'*

'Yes, it's really funny.'

That is so hard to believe as to be laughable. Delia Thomas is an odd, quiet geekette, *surely*? Jeepers, you think you know someone, and then . . .

'I'll walk around with you,' I say. 'I'd love a look at what's going on.'

The queue is the longest snaking line of people I have ever seen in my life, and that includes the queue for Santa in the shopping centre when I was a kid. It's going

---

* I seem to be shouting.

to take hours for Delia to get to the top of it but she doesn't seem too bothered about that.

'We'll take it in turns to go get drinks and ice creams,' she says with a shrug.

If I sneak away and join a bit later, I will be even further back and it'll take even longer for me to get seen. My resolve is wavering, and it wasn't all that strong to begin with. I hear some lads laughing and, when I look ahead to where the sound is coming from, I see my brother's familiar head above the crowd. Right then he turns around and spots me, and I have no choice but to acknowledge him. He looks surprised but beckons me over.

'I'll be back in a minute,' I say to Delia and Maya and then wander over, feeling slightly dazed.

'Hey there, lil Jenser,' Dermot says and ruffles my hair (ARGH, it took me ages to get it looking tousled but not frizzy and he's probably ruined that now).

'What are you doing here?' I ask.

'Obvious, really, sis, trying out for the Big Time.'

He's with a *proper* gang of lads (i.e. more than three) and they all have guitars.

'You know the guys,' he says. 'There are ten of us and we're called . . . guess . . .'

'Ten Guitars?' I chance.

'Bingo!'

'If we all play the same thing at the same time, it'll be awesome.'

Stevie Lee is right in front of me and I could swoon. I get a bit dizzy instead.

'Hey, lil dudette,' he says.

I wish they'd let go of the 'little' thing. OK, I might not be as tall as other girls of my age or older,[†] but don't rub it in.

'Are you trying out?' Dermot asks.

I snort and try to look dismissive. 'No *way*, I just wanted a look.'

'You should, you know, you have a good voice,' he says.

He hasn't been this nice to me in yonks and I get a lump in my throat. I'm a bit hot and bothered that SLB has heard this, though, as I'd prefer to keep my supposed talent under wraps until such time as I know if it's any good at all.

And then I hear a yippedy bark that I recognize[‡] and

[†] or even some who are younger, for that matter.

[‡] It's like some weird, sonic radar I have developed over the years.

I know, without even looking round, that Gypsy is in town and right behind me.

'Wehay!' Dermot is giving a high five to someone I can't yet see.

I turn around and there are Gypsy, Uggs and Dixie. Dermot was high-fiving Uggs and not the mutt, thank goodness.

'We thought you'd need support,' Dixie says. Before I splutter anything totally and utterly and untakeback-ably embarrassing, she adds, 'Gypsy's idea.'

I quickly check that none of the Ten Guitars have heard that, or my cover is blown, but they're so engrossed with being deadly cool that they haven't, so I can breathe a sigh of relief on that slim level.

In other news, my life has just gone down the can.

THE FEAR

'I'm really touched, you know that, but I can't let you stay with me,' I explain. 'I don't mean to be ungrateful, it's just that this is going to take hours and I'll get tetchy and I'll pick fights with you and that won't be fair on you and then we'll fall out even worse than we have already.'

There, I think that about covers everything.

Dixie isn't even listening; she's watching the television cameras. The programme interviews various saddos in the queue and I am determined not to be one of them. I don't want anyone knowing that I was once insane enough to think I could do this, and then went further with the madness and turned up to audition.

The presenter is hyping the crowd up to scream and go wild and she's asking who everyone is and then – oh no, oh, absolutely no blinkin WAY, no, nono – she's seen Gypsy and she's approaching to talk to us.

'Who's this little creature here?' she's asking. 'Can we get a shot of this little cutie?'

Gypsy is in a frenzy of leaping and barking, like she knows she's going to be on television.

I hear Dixie say, 'Hi, I'm Dixie Purvis and I'm here with my friend . . .' She looks round but I'm gone. I'm hiding behind a huge guy with a tuba so I won't be safe for long – novelty items always turn up on the show and a tuba is not an instrument you meet every day on the street.

'Our friend is doing stand-up,' I hear Maya say, approaching the camera crew.

I peek round the tuba and see Delia Thomas has put on specs and is talking to the camera. It's like she's taken on a completely different character, but it's kooky and funny.

'Yeah, Val, I'm trying out,' she's saying to the presenter. 'I'm going to talk about my life and how impossible it is. Like, my dog ate a big chunky corner of my French grammar book,' (Gypsy jumps up and down on cue!), 'so now I'll never know the verb "to give" or how to

213

conjugate it – French people are going to think I'm a deeply selfish person.' She shrugs. 'What can you do? It's like wearing glasses, people think no guy will ever make a pass at you – not so, they *practise* their lines on girls like me and that's good, up to a point – trouble is I can see them clearly because of the specs, so that balances things up, too much really.'

She's really got a good patter and everyone around us is laughing and I realize I have nothing to match that. Singing, as I plan to do, is different and can't be compared, but I know it's not *special* because I haven't written my own song, for example, and from where I am* Delia does have something unusual and good. My throat starts to ache and close in. I don't feel well.

The camera crew move on and I sneak back to my friends. Dixie has slotted us into the queue with Delia and Maya, as if that was where we were to be all along. I thought the twenty minutes earlier waiting for the bus was long, but no, THIS is what a long time means. We shuffle forward for hours and with each step I feel worse and worse. Finally, we make it into the building but it's hotter than hell in here and I think I'm going to

* Hiding behind a brass instrument on the street.

pass out at any minute. We're given numbers and then we wait some more. And more.

Dermot and another nine guitars come out punching the air – they've got a call back. I could not feel more tiny or insignificant. The 'lil' name is apt for me after all.

'Are you OK?' Uggs asks. 'You look really pale.'

I nod, but I'm not convinced I *am* OK. I try to speak but I can't seem to make a sound. Nerves, no doubt. I do my breathing exercises, like we do at choir practice. That feels a bit better.

After waiting for six or seven centuries, *suddenly* we're at the door and Delia is going in – Oh. My. Actual. GOD. I'm next. I do some more breathing but I must be doing it too fast because I get very woozy and have to sit with my head between my legs.

Delia comes out smiling and everyone's voice now sounds like it's coming to me through treacle. She's saying, 'I'm called back,' but it's deep and drawling: 'Eyemcawwwllledbaaaaaaack,' and it's certainly not at the right speed.

A woman with a clipboard grabs me and shoves me through the door going, 'Goooodluuuuuck,' and I'm

inside a big room with a table at the other end and sitting there are Danny Faller (legend and a v v hard man to please), Nicki Richie (singer and professionally fabulous showbiz person) and Tate Goodwin (impresario and top manager). I stagger towards them and try to say my name but my voice won't come. A tiny squeak is all I manage and when I stand in front of them and try to gather myself to sing, the terror is so great that the world goes black and I faint clear away.

When I open my eyes I see a circle of familiar faces leaning over me, all looking very concerned. I am no longer in the Room of Dreams but in a Corridor of Lost Opportunity. The show must go on, it seems, and it has, without me. Thankfully the Ten Guitars are not among the spectators, so I may have escaped Complete and Utter Humiliation.[†]

The woman with the glasses wants me to sign a form which gives permission for the show to use the footage of me fainting through the Fear but Dixie says, 'No way,' and, after an argument, the woman goes away looking

† Although perhaps Stevie Lee would have given me the Kiss of Life . . .

216

The Fear

peeved that they can't broadcast my shame. I'm so glad my friends are here for me.

'I'm sorry, Dixie,' I croak.

'Don't be stupid,' she says.

'Are you going to make fun of me because of this?'

'Of course I am,' she says.

Uggs shakes his head. 'Too soon,' he says to her.

'Yeah, too soon, *NOW*,' she agrees. 'But a time will come.'

I actually manage a small laugh at that and then Gypsy licks my face and I even keep smiling then. Clearly I need medical attention.

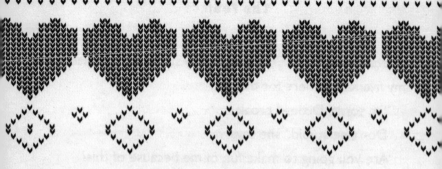

THE SHAME

So, my name should be changed to Jenny Fail. This is the most spectacular mess-up yet. And to think I nearly lost my Bestest Galpal for something that I couldn't even manage to get through without passing out. *EPIC* disazzo. But one that we are keeping to ourselves. Maya and Delia have been sworn to silence, and everyone agrees that what went on at *Teen Factor X* for Jenny 'Failure' Q stays at *Teen Factor X*. I am totally humiliated but relieved that it goes no further.*

Life can move on again with all of the alterations that the latest fail-fest has added to it, but I'm feeling really strange about the whole event. It's like too much spice in a muffin, or too much salt on your chips. Sometimes

* Aside from the torture promised at Dixie's hand when I have recovered enough to feel it more/most.

The Shame

I get a horror flashback. It can come out of nowhere. It's like I'm reliving the audition room beginning to spin and me beginning to wobble and then the blank before I wake to see so many eyes staring down at me. The shame makes me cringe more than the memory of when I fell over and showed my (big) pants. Strangely, I am also relieved that I didn't make it through because I don't think I was ready.[†] But the knock-back has left me with no self-confidence whatsoever and I feel hollow.

The big thing for the Quinns is that Dermot is going to be on TV. Mum and Dad are so excited and proud and I am vaguely sorry that I couldn't add to that by being chosen too, even if I am also now v v glad that I was not.

It's half-term holidays and Dad decides to throw a celebratory barbeque, even though the weather is quite nippy. Ten Guitars are the special guests. It means there are a lot of wrapped-up-warmly guys in the garden giving tips over the flames and burning food, both of which they seem to like to do. I doubt any of them really knows all that much about cooking with fire. I eat too

---

† Well, OK, clearly I wasn't.

219

much houmous and I know I REEK of garlic so I'm feeling v v self-conscious as a result. It seems I don't need a worst enemy as long as I am still breathing[‡] myself!

Then we go indoors and Ten Guitars play some tunes. They're really, *really* good, I think. I am boiling due to the adjacent presence of Stevie Bolton. I'd say I look like a lobster with orange frizzy hair, but I am grinning away and enjoying the performance.

Of course, I think SLB looks coolest and is the best guitar player in the group but I'm also chuffed that my brother seems to be the leader and the one who came up with the whole idea. Then Stevie Lee winks at me and I swallow air so quickly I get hiccoughs. *Très* undignified. I also hope I wasn't staring at him or dribbling and that maybe that's why he winked, like telling someone they have a bogey in their nostril or some of their lunch still on their face.

I wish I had the guts to do a song but I don't. And right now I am only able to make 'hic' noises anyhow. I may never sing in public ever again. I'll hide at the back of the school choir. When Ten Guitars finish we all clap

‡ Fuming, honking, stinky breaths!

220

and then I make my way to the kitchen for emergency chocolate. Mum is telling one of the Oakdale mums her due date and I am reminded that life is about to change for us Quinns. I discover that the two Kit Kats that were there this morning are gone, but instead of being annoyed I start to feel hopeful that Baby Quinn might have something in common with me after all.

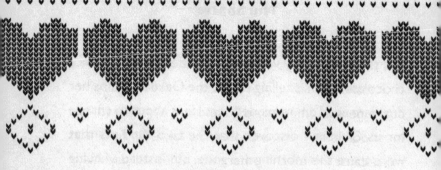

CORNERED

Finally some good news. We got a big order for DA BOMB from the other Slinkies. We've decided to charge two euros a bomb but we may go into making smaller ones so that customers have a choice and can buy one for a euro if they're cash-strapped.

Actually I can't wait for us to sell these bath bombs because we've invested our spare and sparse cash in them and we need to start seeing some returns now. As a result, we've decided this will be our last batch till the initial stock is sold off. I'm getting into the lingo of commerce with 'tradeables' and 'collateral' and all sorts that I don't understand but love the sound of.

We're running low on bicarbonate of soda, so one of us will have to go to the shopping centre for more. We have a system in the Gang when something needs to be done that no one wants to do, like whose turn it is to make the coffee. On a count of three we all point at the person who should go and the person with the most points at them is chosen. Today, even I point at me because I know the others will, as it's still payola for not telling Dix about *Teen Factor X*.

I'm not expecting more MAJOR incidents in my life, because surely I have exhausted all avenues of excitement with fainting at a national event and so on, but things happen, I've learned that much. I am rounding the corner at speed into the shopping centre when I see Mike Hussy, but I'm going at such a lick I can't stop. We nearly collide and are then left staring into each other's face, a nasty experience for both of us if his face is anything to go by. He's got a black eye and his arm is in a sling, which is surprising. I don't remember him being the one flung into oncoming traffic the day he attempted to murder Teddy, intentionally or otherwise.

'Jennifer Quinn,' he says, and it's true, because I am. So, first strike to Hussy.

'Mike,' I say, equally factually.

Evens.

223

Then we just stand there staring at one another. There's not a lot more to say or do.

'I still don't like you,' he tells me. 'But you shopping me to Mr Bradley was good.'

I am probably doing my impression of a puzzled gold-fish but I say, 'Glad to be of help,' with a dollop of irony added in, I hope, because the last thing I really want is to be *helping* this twerp.

'Mum finally kicked my dad out,' he says.

I really don't know why he's telling me this. I don't want to know about his life, I don't like him.

'Well, not before . . .' He shrugs and makes to go.

And then something occurs to me as I look at him limp away and it's as if time stills all around me.

Oh. My. Actual.

I take in his injuries again and I think: 'His dad beat him.'

That's so wrong. Actually, it's criminal. It kind of explains stuff about Mike, though. I am shocked and I feel really gutted for having had any part in it.

'See you when you're back at school,' I say to his back.

He turns round, so I give him a half-smile. He sort of smiles back, and says, 'Guess so, Ginger.'

GINGER?!?! Oh, that hurts.

 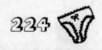

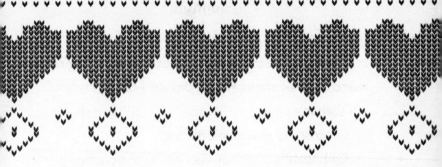

FRIENDS VS FIENDS

Friendship is a strange thing. I wonder where it comes from. Why do we need friends when we have family? Or maybe I should ask, why don't family do as friends? Of course, you can be friends with your family, but it's a different kind of thing, isn't it? You have family from the start that you're born into, from when you can't remember because you're too tiny. But you make friends along the way.

I'm sitting with Dixie at Knit 'n' Knatter, and Uggs hasn't yet arrived. She's doing her cushion cover and she goes, 'Jen . . .' and something in her tone makes me fear the worst.

'Dix . . .' I say, with *trepidation*.

'You know the *Teen Factor X* stuff?'

Oh NO, *not that*, I so don't want to talk about

that.* It was weeks ago now. But I'm expecting to be taken to task about what I did, so I brace myself.

'Yeah . . .'

'I know why you didn't tell me.'

'Oh! Yeah?'

'I understand why you couldn't.'

'You do?'

'Yeah. I would have made fun of you. But not because I don't think you could have done it, more cos that's what I do, that's what I do when I don't know what to do. I'm not very imaginative.'

'Wow,' I say.

'I know!' she says. 'This is me being nearly as mature as Uggs is!'

We both cover our ears and shriek, 'AAAAGGGH-HHH!' to maturity and how it might have infected us.

'We're THIRTEEN,' I squeal. 'TOO SOON.'

Which is when Uggs walks in. And without thinking, or asking why, he just joins in, puts his hands over his ears and goes, 'AAAAAGGGHHHH!' as well.

You have loyalty to family but also to friends. That's

---

* I am a coward and I want to hide from excruciating stuff.

what I was lacking when I hid my plans from Dixie. But it's good that she could see why. I probably should have trusted her, though. I was a coward. We've both learned a lot about ourselves from this, I think.

She's still going to mock me but at least now I know it's meant with love, and a lot of carelessness. And she knows I'm over-sensitive and an eejit. Friends are just fiends with 'r' thrown into the mix – it's a fine line between the two if you don't respect that, I ponder to myself.

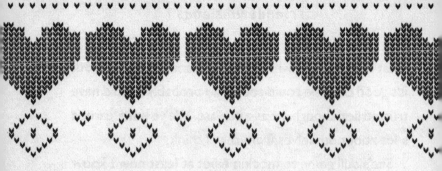

HEROES

Mike Hussy is back to school after his suspension. The place held its breath on the morning of his return but he toed the line. Then, when the teachers stopped watching him so closely, he let loose again. He's not physically pushing people around any more = good, but he's still giving people mega-verbals = non-good. All is not as bad as it used to be, so it's all degrees of improvement and a long way to go to perfection* but, hey, that's life.

One *atrocious* habit he's got into is referring to me as 'the ginger nut'. I am dealing with this through the medium of ignoring it. I pretend it never happened. It's only a matter of time, though, before it gets heard and sticks and then I will be proper cross, but I don't know

* or even 'OK'.

what to do about it. I want to shout, 'SHUT THE FRONT DOOR' at him, but that would draw attention to the nickname, which is the last thing I want. This is v v vexing and not LOL *at all*.

Thankfully, everyone is in a fever of excitement about *Teen Factor X* because Oakdale's finest will be on TV. It's all anyone can talk about, so they're distracted from Mike Hussy and ginger nuts. The Slinkies are total (and official) groupies now to Ten Guitars and the envy of every female in the neighbourhood. I'm family to one of the group and that makes me an honorary groupie, so hurrah for that. I feel part of the adventure and that's great because it involves v little participation[†] on my part. I simply add a lot of enthusiasm.

People are treating Delia with a bit of awe too. No one knew she could be funny, though I think she's getting a bit cheesed off with nerds going, 'Tell us a joke, Delia.' She says she doesn't 'do' jokes, which is way cool and v up to the minute comedy-wise. Lots of people think it might just be a spoof that a quiet girl in our class is going to be on the show. When she's not in her stand-up

---

† Just as well, considering what happened when I did actually try to take part!

229

character, Delia is forgettable and odd. I think she likes it that way.

Everything's barrelling along at a slick pace. Best of all is we're taking orders for DA BOMB and, because a Slinky mum is having a birthday and has ordered fifty mini bombs to give to her guests, we are finally making our money back. PHEW!

Mum's bump is HUGE now too. Her latest jars of pickles have whole tomatoes and bits of cauliflower in them and look even more like samples from a laboratory. Gran keeps asking if she's having twins and Mum says no and Gran says maybe one is hiding behind the other when the scans are taken. This is a v worrying idea. I have come to terms with the notion of having one baby arriving into our world, NOT two – that would be like an invasion by a tiny, crying, pooping army.

I'm more nervous than I should be about seeing the Dublin trials of *Teen Factor X* on TV. Basically, I am still v worried that the show might have some footage of me keeling over that's usable without my permission and that it'll SO be recognizable as me that I will JUST DIE or have to run away from home and, in fact, Ireland.

It's not like I can earn a living from busking on the streets of Europe or America, seeing as I seem to have a fear of performing solo. I can barely eat a second Kit Kat before the Quinns gather to see Dermot in glory on our nation's screens.

It's weird watching something that I remember. I'm there again but I'm not[‡] and I'm hoping I won't relive all the horror of the day. There's the long line of hopefuls weaving down the streets, shots of screaming teens and then suddenly Gypsy is on the screen, barking, and we give a big cheer. Dixie is speaking to the camera (another cheer) and then Delia is saying funny words, and Uggs and Maya are grinning loons, and if you look v v closely at the foot area of the guy holding the tuba you just MIGHT recognize my floaty skirt.

No one here at home notices it but I get a text from Dixie: **I c ur on tv!**

I go: **my bum is big in that skirt**. And she sends: **HUMUNGUS!**

We see some losers being a bit tragic, including a

‡ i'm on the home sofa, obvs.

231

kid my age singing well off-key[6] and I cringe a lot for her. She puts in a hundred notes where one would do, the sort of thing Mariah Carey can *just about* get away with. She is convinced she's fabuloso and argues her case when she's told she is not getting a call back.

'You could easily do that,' Gran says, and I kind of fob it off with a moody shrug, but not too much because I don't want this to be a discussion. For all I know, Gran is referring to the arguing and not the so-called singing. Luckily for me, just then, our ten teenage heroes enter the room on-screen, armed with guitars, and we give a huge whoopy cheer. Dermo is morto.

'Ooh, don't you look handsome,' Mum says.

'Big nose,' I say, though not with a mean tone.

'No, it's not,' Mum says.

'Yeah, it is,' I say and he thumps me with a cushion. I can tell he's thrilled with how he and all the guys look.

It's magic to see them on television. They play really well and there are lots of shots of Stevie Lee looking totally lush.[§] Then there's loads of praise from the judges and Ten Guitars go through and we all punch

6 That could have been me!!!

§ I swear he could make a stone go weak.

the air at the same time as the lads do on TV. It's strange to see Dermot here in the lounge and there on the box. MAD!

Delia is up next and she's great and the Quinns laugh a lot at her and when she goes through we punch the air again. Then there's some stuff that makes my heart freeze over. The presenter says it doesn't go so well for everyone and there are some shots of a kerfuffle and the camera jostles to see someone being carried out, but the Fainter isn't seen. Then we see the judges laughing so hard they have tears in their eyes and Nicki says, 'That poor little girl. And she looked so cute with her lovely red hair, then all of a sudden she was totally conked out.'

RED hair? Ah, here now! 'Strawberry blonde!!' I want to shout, but I can't without giving myself away.

And it wasn't THAT funny, thank you very much.

'Aw, the poor little thing,' Mum says.**

This is galling but at least my cover isn't blown, so I'll have to put up with such slurs as being referred to as ginger and a titch.

The excitement must be catching, too much for Mum, because she's looking very pale. Then Dad gets

** Again with the 'little'!

233

concerned. She's clenching her eyes shut in pain.

'What's wrong, Vic?' Dad asks.

'I don't know,' she whispers, and she looks afraid.

Time slows to a full stop. We're all trying to figure out what's going on, especially Mum. Finally she says, 'It's the baby,' and we all try to look like we have a plan of action. We don't. We're just moving about for the sake of it, as if that will help. But what no one wants to say is that Bumpy Quinn isn't due yet. Our baby is coming way too early.

Then Dad snaps to and takes charge.

'I'll get the car,' he says. 'Help Vic out,' he instructs Gran and Dermot.

'Should we not call an ambulance?' Gran says.

'No time,' Dad says.

I gather bags and keys and so on, not really knowing what we need for this unexpected journey. I follow, feeling useless. Mum is put gently into the front seat, Dad gets behind the wheel and the rest of the Quinns pile into the back.

Mum keeps saying, 'Sorry, Dermot, I don't mean to ruin your night. You were so good. Well done.' It's almost like a mantra, a verse to keep her going.

It's too early for her to be having the baby and we're

all terrified, you can practically taste it in the air as we rush to the hospital and all silently, fervently, pray our prayers.

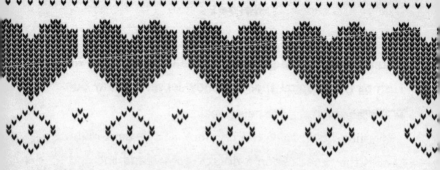

EMERGENCY

Gran leaps out of the car* and rushes to get a wheelchair and help. Dad tells Dermot to park the car – I didn't even know my brother could drive. Mum is rushed up to the maternity ward with Dad and we're left in the Accident and Emergency surrounded by patients on trolleys and slumped in chairs, some groaning and some bleeding. There is a strong whiff of disinfectant, and a feeling of chaos in the place, and a lot of other stuff I don't want to think about or identify.

Gran consults with some nurses then ushers us to the stairs, saying that the lifts are for patients and medical staff and not day-trippers like us. The family waiting room is on the maternity level, four floors up, so that's eight flights of stairs and it takes us quite a while to huff

* She can sure move at speed when she wants to!

and puff up. I'm sure Gran has done this deliberately to keep us occupied and also out of the way while more important matters are being dealt with.

We find Dad pacing the corridor and he says Mum is with the nurse. Then a doctor comes and she and Dad both disappear through a door. It's agony not knowing what's going on and I want to cry, but we have to be strong for Mum, and for one another, now.

What if something is wrong with our baby? It's terrifying to think of that. What if Mum is in danger? I have never been so scared in my life. Time passes more slowly than it ever has before, slower than very slow motion, yet my heart is beating faster than it ever has and I am gasping for breath but trying not to show it. I notice that Dermot's hands are shaking and Gran's eyes look very moist.

Dad comes back and says the baby is in distress so they're preparing Mum for an operation to deliver the baby by Caesarean section. We can go and see her now for a minute before she goes to theatre.

Mum is in the last bed in a ward full of women. She looks pale and scared but she forces herself to smile at us.

'Don't worry,' she says. 'It'll all be OK. The little varmint is coming early and out through the sun roof, no less.'

237

I think they might have given her something already because she's sort of slurring her words and if this wasn't such a serious situation, that would be almost funny.

She clutches Gran's hand and Gran goes, 'You'll be fine, darling, and so will baby.'

'I hope so,' Mum whispers.

I realize I love Bumpy Quinn and I want to meet Bumpy in person and for everything to be all right. My heart might break right now at the thought that anything could go wrong.

This is the most frightening time of my life. I want to help but I don't know what would be good to do and what would be disastrous. Everything is so quiet you can practically hear the hum of our panic. I don't know why, but I start to sing. It's 'I'd Do Anything', a number from *Oliver!* that Mum and I often change the words to. This time I sing it for real and do her part too.

Mum smiles and I think she looks a bit less worried. Dermot and Gran look impressed and I don't even care that all the women in the ward are staring at me. When I finish they even applaud me![†]

† Blushmost!

Emergency

As Mum is being wheeled away, she says, 'I'll be back for another of those as soon as I can, Jen.'

I feel like I've done something good, something useful, but it doesn't ease the awful worry.

Then, the agonizing wait begins. It feels like hours but, in fact, Baby Harry is born twenty minutes later. He is put in an incubator because he is early and so small – only five pounds, Gran says, and I think she means two and a bit kilos. We are allowed to look at him through a glass partition and he is the most beautiful baby I have ever seen. I know everyone says that about their baby but Harry really, really is GORGEOUS.

He's curled up in a little ball with his fists pressed against his face, sleeping off his dramatic arrival into the world. He has dark hair and I am relieved we don't have another strawberry blonde in the family. Dad puts his hand beside the baby so we can see just how small he is. That's my baby brother right there. I want to run through every room in the hospital and tell everyone I meet about Harry Quinn, who has already made a big mark on the world, our world, my world.

We go and see Mum and there are hugs and tears and we all tell her how well she's done. Harry is healthy

239

and strong, Dad says, and he'll be out of the incubator and ready to go home before we know it. SO, there's shopping to be done, because he's here sooner than expected and we are *sooo* not prepared.

I can't wait to get him home and hold him. And make sure that Gypsy doesn't think he's her new plaything.

I text Uggs and Dixie: **baby harry arrived early i.e. tonight!**

Dix goes: **NO WAY – HRA!**

Uggs: **WOW! CONGRATS.**

Just when I think there'll be no message from Gypsy I get: **WOOF!**‡

Dermot looks at the floor, red-faced. 'Harry must have hated Ten Guitars if his response was to get born early.'

'Or maybe the opposite,' Mum says. 'He might have got fed up of waiting to get out and about and start being a star like his big brother and sister.'

Then it hits home – I'm still the only Quinn girl! Smiley face.

---

‡ It makes me laugh, though I'll never admit that to the Gang.

 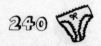

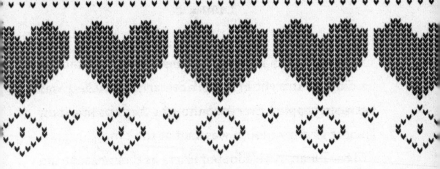

YULE DO

Christmas in our house smells of baby and plum pudding. Mum didn't get a chance to do proper nesting, as she calls it, before Harry arrived, so she's making up for it now. She and Harry spent a few weeks in the hospital while they checked he was OK and let him grow a little bit more. Now Mum's gone v v domestic. There are happy consequences to this, one of which is brilliant dinners in the evenings.* Harry's being breastfed,† so whatever Mum eats is filtered through her for him. He still appreciates a Kit Kat, though what he deposits in his nappies converts them into weapons of mass destruction.

* And she's done with pickles, which is a relief - I so don't get vinegar.
† Dad calls it 'on draught', which makes me, like, TOTALLY squirm.

I am actually quite good at changing him now, though he did pee straight into my face early on while I was between nappies. Everyone thought that was hilarious. I'm just glad my mouth was shut at the time.

Ten Guitars have adopted Harry as their mascot and they visit him all the time because they say he brings them good luck. They've gone through to the next round of *Teen Factor X* and they say it's all because Harry took such an interest in them that he came out early to support them. Which means I am seeing a lot of SLB. That's great but it means my nerves are constantly shredded at the thought that he might appear at any moment.

Also, I spend a lot of the day praying, to any power in the universe that might listen, that Mum won't be feeding Harry when any of the group is around. I know it's natural and all that, but she's my MUM and those are her BOOBS on show!‡

Christmas is almost upon us and there is much to be done in the Quinn household. A strange thing happened last week when we put up the decorations around the house. Someone put mistletoe over the front door

‡ I wonder if I am a prude?

without telling. I suspect Gran, because it's exactly the kind of mischief she likes to unleash. I was inside the door when Uggs came through it and he saw the mistletoe and gave me a kiss. But he deliberately did lips on lips. And it was OK. No tongues, so not wet. Not unpleasant either. Odd because it was Uggs, but, yeah, OK. Then we pretended it never happened. And that's how things will stay.

Gypsy jumped up and down looking for attention but I refused to let her kiss me. A girl has to draw the line somewhere and that cur is not to be encouraged. Next thing she'll think I like her, which I do not.

Dixie *so* got the Uggs kiss out of me and I'll never be let forget it, but she also thinks the mistletoe should be used to my advantage re Stevie Lee. Her plan is that I lurk by the front door for the entire festive season. That would be a great idea if there weren't so many of Dermot's friends coming through the house and the chances of being snogged by an eejit pal of his are therefore way too great.

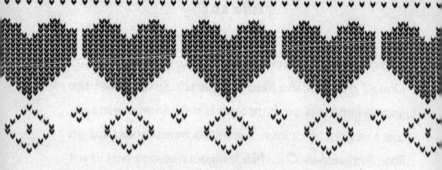

CHRISTMAS DAY

My gifts are a total hit (MEGAPHEW!). I have added a tiny stripy hat for Harry, like Dermot's but much smaller. I get a great picture of both of them wearing the Jenny Q Collection for Young Men. I've also embroidered words on a bib for him, so it says BURP MACHINE. I get fairy lights from Mum and Dad, just what I wanted for my room, and a brilliant calligraphy set from Gran and a totally cool T-shirt from Dermot with an illustration of ten guitars on it that he got made especially for me. Dixie is SO going to see a merchandising opportunity there.

If Ten Guitars get through to the next stage of *Teen Factor X*, Dermot says he might wear his Jenny Q creation on television!!!!

Maybe the other nine will want one?

Maybe I'll be knitting for SLB!

Christmas Day

YIKES.

The day after Christmas, Stevie Lee actually visits with a gift for Harry, and I am under the mistletoe so I get a peck on the cheek. I am so startled I move to one side and accidentally brush my lips against his (!). I nearly faint.* It is v v brief contact and lovely, I am happy to report, though it kind of burns me due to my passion for him.

Dermot is beside me and SLB says, 'Love you, mate, but no tongues,' to him and they hug and do a blokey, funny peck.

I haven't been able to speak to SLB since. Well, nothing beyond 'Lo', which is as close to 'hello' as I can manage without falling over. This lurve stuff is v draining.

I'm sitting on the sofa planning some baby knits and thinking about the year and how I freaked when I heard I was going to have a new brother or sister, and how selfish I was to only think about how that looked for me. Who cares how things *look*?† That's not what's important. I couldn't be prouder of the Quinn family

* I hope I haven't gone all blotchy and stupid-looking.

† Admittedly big pinky knickers will probably never look good . . . on anyone.

right now. And I think I've learnt how to trust those closest to me a bit better too. I nearly lost Dixie through not trusting her, and Uggs through trusting him too much with information he didn't need or want.

Maybe we're all like a piece of knitting. Gran says it's our mistakes along the way that make us unique. As long as we learn from them, we'll be stronger, better, and they'll have been worth making, as painful as they may sometimes be. It's good to know mistakes are OK. Nothing is perfect.

Except for baby Harry Quinn, of course.

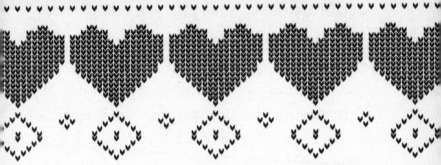

If you want to learn to knit like me,

Jenny Q,*

then here's how!

*As taught by the master teacher Dixie, of course!

DAD'S SKINNY TIE

I'm using one 50g ball of bright (lime) green double-knit cotton (same as I'm using on Dermot's hat) on 5mm needles.

Cast on 10 stitches – this should lead to a tie 4 cm wide, but you can make it thinner by having less stitches (say two less) or wider, with more stitches, depending on your taste.

Knit 1, purl 1, every row, until it measures 150 cm in length.

BUT: a Quinn Tip (or **Q TIP!**) = slip the first stitch of every row (i.e. do not knit it but pass it on to the needle you're knitting and purling on to) and then continue as per instructions and this gives a lovely edge on both long sides of the tie.

Cast off.
Hide the tail of the yarn by sewing it up the side.

RESULT = one bright, skinny tie.

GRAN'S FINGERLESS MITTENS

The purple yarn I chose is perfect for Gran because her party piece is a poem about how to grow old wearing purple and learning to spit – it's v funny, and v worrying because she does wear purple, though I'm not sure if she has spat at anyone recently. She is definitely growing older. In this case I'm going to say that two out of three ain't bad and will certainly do if the spitting is left out.

I ran up a tension square using the purple cashmere mix on 5mm needles and my measurements on that are: **9 stitches = 4 cm, and 11 rows = 4 cm**.

So, knit two identical pieces, one for each hand, and they'll be interchangeable. Only two stitches are used **= plain/knit** and **purl**.

Cast on 36 stitches (so the pieces will be 16 cm wide). Knit the first 8 rows – this will give a nice textured edge that won't roll up.

Then switch to knit I row, purl I row, until the piece is 24 cm in length.

Knit the final 8 rows, for a matching upper edge, and cast off.

Repeat.

To make up

Simply sew the sides of each piece together with a wool needle (these needles are special and blunt so they don't split the yarn) and the same yarn as you've knitted with.

Go up 18 cm and finish off.

Then leave a gap of 4 cm (for the thumb).

Sew the rest up to the top.

Neaten any stray lengths of yarn.

Twice.

Hey presto, Luxury Mittens!

MUM'S COWL/SNOOD

I'm using two balls of bobbledy yarn (a kind called 'Splendour' that goes through two shades of pink to mauve and purple), four balls of chunky purple wool and 10mm needles.

Using the textured yarn of your choice (to make a frilly, luxurious edge for wearing up over the head like a hood), cast on 90 stitches (this is the painful part of using this yarn – it takes a while to cast on and knit the first row!). Also, these needles are so big it sometimes feels like I'm knitting with huge, pointy sticks, which I am, I guess.

Knit 1 row, purl 1 row, until you have used up the two balls.

Switch to the plain wool and continue to knit 1 row, purl 1 row, until it measures, say, 40 cm in length. You want it to have a roomy, hoody look when it's worn up on the head and not be skimpy and stretched.

Then knit 1, purl 1, for 6 rows to make a nice ribbed finish that won't curl back on itself.

Sew the two sides together with the purple yarn and a wool needle and neaten off any loose yarn.

VOILA! A lovely luxurious snood.

DERMOT'S STRIPY HAT

This will take one ball of black double-knit cotton and some of the bright green I'm also using for Dad's Skinny Tie, on 5mm needles.

My tension for this is:
14 stitches and 14 rows = 7 cm × 7 cm.

Cast on 84 stitches in black.

Knit 1 row, purl 1 row, for 8 rows in black. This will curl up and give a nice bottom edge to the hat.

Switch to green and knit 1 row, purl 1 row.

Back to the black and knit 1 row, purl 1 row, twice.

SO: it's 2 rows green, 4 rows black, from now on. Continue till the piece measures 13 cm, then things get 'interesting' because we're going to start shaping the top of the hat which means decreasing stitches!

(Knit 18, knit 2 together) 4 times, knit 4 = now you should have 80 stitches.

Purl 4, purl 2 together, (purl 17, purl 2 together) 3 times, purl 17 = 76 stitches.

(I'll use abbreviations now, because that's what other patterns will always have, so K is knit, P is purl, K2tog = knit 2 together, P2tog = purl 2 together.)

(K16, K2tog) 4 times, K4 = 72 stitches.

P4, P2tog, (P15, P2tog) 3 times, P15 = 68 stitches.

(K14, K2tog) 4 times, K4 = 64 stitches.

P4, P2tog, (P13, P2tog) 3 times, P13 = 60 stitches.

(K12, K2tog) 4 times, K4 = 56 stitches.

P4, P2tog, (P11, P2tog) 3 times, P11 = 52 stitches.

(K10, K2tog) 4 times, K4 = 48 stitches.

P4, P2tog, (P9, P2tog) 3 times, P9 = 44 stitches.

(K8, K2tog) 4 times, K4 = 40 stitches.

P4, P2tog, (P7, P2tog) 3 times, P7 = 36 stitches.

(K6, K2tog) 4 times, K4 = 32 stitches.

P4, P2tog, (P5, P2tog) 3 times, P5 = 28 stitches.

(K4, K2tog) 4 times, K4 = 24 stitches.

P4, P2tog, (P3, P2tog) 3 times, P3 = 20 stitches.

Then cut the yarn and use a wool needle to thread it through these 20 stitches and fasten it off.

Sew up the sides = one stripy beanie hat!

v v v v v v v v v v v v v v v v v v v v v v v v v v v v v v v v v v v v

HARRY'S 'PIXIE' HAT

This is kind of a mirror image of Dermot's hat because I have used the same two colours of yarn but there's more green than black in Harry's.

It's knit 1 row, purl 1 row, as per Dermot's hat, so it's stocking stitch again.

Cast on 36 stitches in green.

(Knit 1 row, purl 1 row) 3 times = 6 rows.

Switch to black for 2 rows.
Green for 4 rows.
Black for 2 rows.
Green for 4 rows.
Black for 2 rows.

Then, in green, K5, K2tog, (K4, K2tog) 4 times, K5 = 31 stitches.
Purl 1 row.
K3, K2tog, (K4, K2tog) 4 times, K2 = 26 stitches.
Purl 1 row.

In black, K2, K2tog, (K3, K2tog) 4 times, K2 = 21 stitches.
Purl 1 row.
In green, (K2, K2tog) 5 times, K1 = 16 stitches

Cast off and sew along the seam with right sides facing
one another.

Turn inside out and you've got a Harry hat!

Oh, all right, *SHEESH*! Here's the pattern for

GYPSY'S COAT

I'm only adding it because it'll make Uggs happy . . .
Uggs used an Aran weight pure wool on 5mm needles
and his tension square was:
17 stitches and 24 rows = 10 cm.

It's in three pieces: a top, a bottom, and a hood section.
I know, I know, he knitted her a *hood* on her coat too
= **MADNESS!** And this will only fit a v small dog –
a runty sized mutt.

TOP

Cast on 46 stitches.

Knit 6 rows.

Then knit 1 row, purl 1 row, until the piece measures
23 cm long.

Knit 6 rows and cast off.

BOTTOM

Cast on 20 stitches.

Knit 6 rows.

Then knit 1 row, purl 1 row, until the piece measures 18 cm long.

Knit 6 rows and cast off.

HOOD

Cast on 30 stitches.

Knit 1 row, purl 1 row.

Continue to knit 1 row, purl 1 row, but increase by a stitch at each end of every knit row. (How you do this is K1, then lift the low loop between this and the next stitch on to the left-hand needle and knit it too, so you have created a new stitch.)

Keep going till you have 46 stitches.
Purl 1 row.

Cast off.

vvvvvvvvvvvvvvvvvvvvvvvvvvvvvvvvvvvvvvv

TO MAKE UP

Put the top and bottom sections with right sides facing together (one piece will be longer than the other), then, starting at the 'neck', stitch along each side for 5 cm, leave a gap of 5 cm (for the mutt's legs) and continue to join the rest to the end. Turn it 'right way' out.

With right sides together, attach the shortest edge of the hood to the collar bit of the coat, then (right sides together) do up the final seam, which will give the hood its shape.

Thusly, you have **one barktastic dog coat** . . . or a barking mad garment, if you ask me.

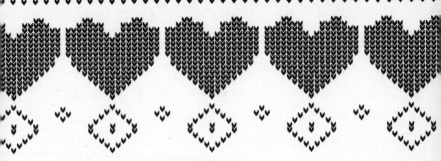

I'm lucky to have Dixie to show me how to do stuff and, if you can at all, it's v great to get someone who can knit to help and to show you how to do the stitches – and how to calm down when things go wrong! There are good books out there too that are v helpful – one is *Purls of Wisdom* by Jenny Lord (published by Penguin Books) and it has illustrations, which are the next best things to having a living knitting guru with you in person.*

* Never tell Dixie I called her something good, she'd never let me forget it!

ACKNOWLEDGEMENTS

A big shout out to those who let me use their names in some way – especially Uggs Grundy, Gypsy Carman, Dan Nightingale, Steve Bolton, Vic and Doug. Thanks to Lawrence Till for letting me use one of his favourite put-downs. Orla Shortall does not bite her nails, Peter Gowen does play guitar brilliantly and Hugo Pheiffer has not (yet) been vommed on in public (phew!). Paddy O'Doherty gave lots of great tips and direction when Jenny's story was emerging, as well as Shannon Park and Wendy Shakespeare at Puffin, and Daphne Tagg. Sam Combes is the brillo designer who made this book look SO good. As always, Richard Cook and Faith O'Grady have been brilliant support. Thanks to my mum, Sheila, for teaching me to knit. HOORAY for the lot of you!

It all started with a Scarecrow.

Puffin is seventy years old.

Sounds ancient, doesn't it? But Puffin has never been
so lively. We're always on the lookout for the next big
idea, which is how it began all those years ago.

Penguin Books was a big idea from the mind of
a man called Allen Lane, who in 1935 invented
the quality paperback and changed the world.
**And from great Penguins, great Puffins grew,
changing the face of children's books forever.**

The first four Puffin Picture Books were hatched in 1940 and the
first Puffin story book featured a man with broomstick arms called
Worzel Gummidge. In 1967 Kaye Webb, Puffin Editor, started the
Puffin Club, promising to **'make children into readers'**.
She kept that promise and over 200,000 children became
devoted Puffineers through their quarterly instalments of
Puffin Post, which is now back for a new generation.

Many years from now, we hope you'll look back and
remember Puffin with a smile. **No matter what your age
or what you're into, there's a Puffin for everyone.**
The possibilities are endless, but one thing is for sure:
whether it's a picture book or a paperback, a sticker book
or a hardback, **if it's got that little Puffin
on it – it's bound to be good.**